CANDY CANE KILLER

MONA MARPLE

PROLOGUE

It was Christmas Eve, and I was about to close the surgery when there was an authoritative tap on the locked door.

I'd already stepped out of my sensible work shoes and put on my snow boots, ready to trek up the hill to Claus Cottage, and I wondered whether I should change my footwear before greeting whoever was out there.

I decided against the idea, hoping that my footwear would make it clear that the surgery hours were done and I was as ready for the Christmas break as everyone else.

I opened the door, prepared to give a warm welcome to one of the familiar faces of my patients. I swore that some of them made regular appointments purely so they had an excuse to enquire about my wedding plans.

Not that there were any wedding plans, of course.

I'd only been engaged for a short time but already word had spread throughout Candy Cane Hollow, and the number of patients requesting daily appointments had gone through the roof.

And so, my smile as I opened the door was the smile of a

newly engaged woman who had answered 'there's no date set as of yet' at least four million times.

But there, on the doorstep, was not one of my daily patients. Nor was it one of the old women who showered me with home-made bakes more often than was good for my waistline.

My surprise guest was an elderly man, dressed entirely inappropriately for the weather in a three piece suit and brogues.

"Can I help?" I asked, as the snow bucketed down on top of his head. He had surprisingly generous hair but it was stuck to his head in a less than flattering way.

"Please," he said, with a nod towards the waiting room.

I opened the door and allowed him inside, where he made a show of extending each of his limbs in turn as if to bring them back to life after being in the sub-zero temperatures outside.

I tried not to look at the state of the freshly vacuumed carpet.

"Are you needing an appointment? We're closed now for the holidays but I can give you the emergency number," I offered.

He shook his head and lowered his stiff old body into one of the chairs. He seemed in no rush to explain his presence.

I found myself fascinated by the man. Who could have such a leisurely air about them on Christmas Eve?

I had a to do list that was about a mile long, and I was already running an hour later than I'd planned.

"How can I help?" I plastered a smile on my face.

"You are Dr Wood, I can presume?"

"That's me," I gave a nod. "And you are?"

"Peter Rhimes. A pleasure to make your acquaintance. May I look around?"

I was too stunned by the request to object, and before I knew it, the old man was up out of the chair and heading towards the filing cabinets.

"And these are..." he began.

"You can't look in those," I said, although the objection was unnecessary as the cabinets were always locked and the key was stored securely in a safe box that was also locked, and the key for that was... well, let's just say the system was secure.

"Ah. Good. This is your office?"

I nodded. The door to the office was unlocked, because I'd walked out of there to answer the front door. It would be locked when I finally got to leave for the day, which wouldn't appear to be happening any time soon.

I followed Peter into the space.

"Tidy. I approve," Peter said.

"Thank you. Are you looking for a new surgery? Because we could arrange a consultation in the New Year if so."

Peter turned to me sharply. "Do you have somewhere to be?"

I gave a nervous laugh. "I'm happy to help you. I'm just not sure what you're looking for."

He raised an eyebrow at me. "You don't know who I am?"

"Should I?"

"Well, this is refreshing. You know who my client is?"

"I'm afraid I've never heard of you. I have no idea who your client is, but that doesn't really matter. My patients all have confidentiality. I can't tell you anything about whoever your client is. Sorry." I added the last word as it seemed that Peter Rhimes was a man used to getting his way.

He raised an eyebrow and grinned, his smile revealing a mouth largely devoid of teeth. "Excellent."

I shifted from one foot to the other. "I'm afraid I really do have to close up now. You can always put a request in writing and we'll consider it, but we'll need your client's authorisation before we can speak to you about anything."

"You're used to dealing with matters of a sensitive nature?"

"Yes," I said. I was a doctor, of course I was used to dealing with sensitive issues. I'd seen and heard things that most people wouldn't believe, and I couldn't tell a single soul about any of them.

He reached into his blazer and pulled out a slim envelope, which he placed on my desk.

"What's this?" I asked.

"New patient registration forms. All complete," he said.

"Oh! Well, of course. We'd be happy to have you, Mr Rhimes."

He let out a reedy laugh. "Not me, dear. I have no intentions of leaving Harley Street. My client, however, has other plans."

I picked up the envelope and led Mr Rhimes out of my office, back to the waiting area.

"My secretary will be happy to process these papers in the new year. Your client will hear from us soon. In the meantime, here's the emergency number," I handed him a business card with the out of hours details on.

He examined it and placed it in his blazer pocket.

"You've been tremendously helpful, Dr Wood," he said as he pushed the door open and returned out to the frigid cold.

"You're very welcome. Merry Christmas!" I called after

him, but the snow swirled aggressively and his shape was swallowed by the storm within a few moments.

I stood in the doorway, watching the snowflakes dance in the wind. My mind was still reeling from the bizarre encounter with Mr Rhimes. Who was his mysterious client? And what did he want with my practice?

As I turned to head back to my office, my phone buzzed in my pocket. It was my fiancé, Nick. I had a fiancé!

"Hey," I answered, my voice still rattled.

"Is everything okay?" Nick's voice sounded concerned.

"I just had the weirdest visit from a man named Peter Rhimes," I explained, as I stepped back into my office and closed the door behind me.

"Who's he?"

"I have no idea. He didn't say much about himself, but he left me these new patient forms for his client."

"What kind of client?"

"I have no idea. But it feels like something big."

Nick was silent for a moment, and then he spoke again. "Be careful, okay? You never know what kind of people are out there."

I swallowed a laugh. "I can take care of myself."

"I know you can," Nick replied, "but I worry about you. Especially when strange people start showing up at your practice."

"I appreciate your concern, but I'm sure it's nothing. Just some wealthy client who wants to switch to a more exclusive practice."

"Maybe. But just be careful, okay?"

"I will. Love you."

"Love you too."

I hung up the phone and sat down at my desk, staring at

the envelope from Peter Rhimes. There was something about the whole encounter that didn't sit right with me. Maybe it was the way he looked at me, like he knew something I didn't. Or maybe it was the fact that he seemed to be casing my office.

I shook my head, trying to dispel the feeling of unease. It was probably nothing. Just a weird encounter with a strange old man. I opened the envelope and began to review the forms inside, trying to focus on something else.

But as I read through the medical history section, something caught my eye. The client's name was blank. That was strange. I flipped through the rest of the pages, but there was no name or identifying information anywhere on the forms.

My heart began to race as I realised that this was not just a strange encounter, but something more sinister. Who was this mystery client that Peter Rhimes was so protective of?

I picked up the phone and dialed the emergency number I had given to Mr. Rhimes. It rang for what felt like an eternity before a deep voice answered.

"Hello?"

"Hi, this is Dr. Wood. I received some new patient forms from a Peter Rhimes earlier today, but there's no name or identifying information on the forms. I was just wondering if you could tell me who the patient is?"

There was a long pause on the other end of the line before the voice spoke again.

"I'm sorry, doctor. I can't disclose that information."

"But I'm his doctor. I need to know who my patient is in order to properly care for them."

"I understand, doctor. But our client has requested complete confidentiality. We cannot divulge any information about them without their express permission."

I sighed, frustrated. "Can you at least tell me what kind

of medical issue they're experiencing? I need to know how to prepare for their first appointment."

"I'm sorry, doctor. I cannot disclose that information either. All I can say is that it is a sensitive matter and our client trusts your discretion."

I hung up the phone, feeling defeated. It seemed like I was going to have to wait until the mysterious client made an appointment to find out anything more.

But as I sat at my desk, staring at the blank space where the patient's name should have been, I knew that this was not going to be a normal case. Something was off, and I was determined to get to the bottom of it.

1
___

By the time I finally made it up the hill to Claus Cottage, I looked like a walking snowman and was a good ninety minutes later than I'd hoped.

Gilbert opened the door before I'd even reached it, as if he had a sixth sense for someone approaching the property, which I wasn't sure was not the case.

He looked me up and down and let out a sigh. "I can see I'll be busy with the mop again, following after you."

"Nice to see you too, Gilbert," I teased. The house elf had always been fastidious but that had increased to impossible standards ever since Nick had proposed to me at the Winter Ball.

"You're very late," he whispered as he held out his hands to take my coat.

"I know. I'm sorry. Is everyone annoyed with me?"

Gilbert rolled his eyes. "The world doesn't revolve around you, Holly Wood. We've had some very exciting news and that's taken up all of our attention. I haven't even had chance to start dinner yet!"

I widened my eyes with surprise. Gilbert had strong

opinions about the time each meal of the day should be served, and Santa help anyone who was tardy.

"What's happened?" I asked, curious to know whatever had him in such a flap he was not only serving dinner late, but didn't appear at all stressed because of it.

Gilbert grinned gleefully. "Well, I guess I can tell you…"

"Gilbert, let my daughter-in-love in the house! She must be soaked!" Mrs Claus called as she poked her head out of the den.

Gilbert's cheeks flushed at the reprimand. His greatest fear in life was to disappoint Mrs Claus.

"Holly! Whatever kept you so long, dear? I've been telling Nick you really are too kind-hearted with those patients. They'll keep you all night if you let them," Mrs Claus said as she approached, then reached up on her tip toes and planted a kiss on my icy cheek.

"She should really start using a sleigh more, too," Gilbert mumbled.

"That's probably not a bad idea," I admitted with a laugh. "I've been trying to get my steps in to try and counteract some of the…"

I stopped suddenly, but I'd realised my mistake too late. Gilbert's eyes bore into me.

"Were you about to complain about the food?"

"No! Not yours, Gilbert. The trouble is, some people in Candy Cane Hollow don't have your respect for nutritionally balanced meals," I said with a terrified grin plastered across my face.

Gilbert puffed out his chest and stood a little straighter. "Yes, you're absolutely right. And you'll want to be paying very close attention to your food intake now, in the run up to the wedding."

I gave a nervous laugh and felt a desperate urge to

change the subject. "Gilbert, did you say there's news?"

The elf clasped his hands over his mouth and practically broke out into a river dance. It was as if the floor was hot lava. I hadn't seen him in such a state since Glade launched their pumpkin spice latte plug-in air freshener.

"Let's get Holly settled and then you can tell her everything," Mrs Claus insisted.

She led us into the den, not the grand dining room. So it was true; whatever the news was, it had Gilbert excited enough that usual mealtimes had been forgotten. I never thought I'd see the day.

I squeezed in the love seat next to Nick, who leaned over and planted a kiss on my forehead. I swore I heard Mrs Claus swoon.

"You look soaked," Nick said, his voice thick with concern.

"I'll change before dinner. Gilbert said there's some news I'll want to hear?"

Nick smiled, and the dimple in his cheek grinned at me too. Now I was the one swooning.

"Go on, Gilbert, the suspense is killing her," Nick teased. He knew that I was no fan of gossip.

"Well, I heard this direct from Yule Believe It, so you know it's good," Gilbert began.

"Yule Believe It?" I asked. The name was familiar but I couldn't remember why.

"Candy Cane Hollow's greatest journalist," Gilbert gushed.

"It's an online gossip column," Nick clarified in a whisper. He didn't dare say it loud enough for Gilbert to hear.

"Oh, okay," I said.

"You'll never guess who is moving to Candy Cane Hollow?" Gilbert asked, his eyes wide.

"Erm... I have no idea," I admitted as I tried to make my voice reflect some degree of interest.

"Angel!" Gilbert exclaimed. His face broke out into a grin usually reserved for when his custard had the silky glean he always aimed for, and he even indulged in some jazz hands.

"Angel who?" I asked.

"You know, dear, the singer," Mrs Claus said. Her eyes made a desperate plea for me to find some recognition for this person who had our practical, unflappable Gilbert in such a state.

"Oh, the singer! Wow, really?" I decided that bluffing was the safest way though the rest of the conversation.

"Holly and I used to dance to her first song when we were teenagers," August revealed, with a wink. There were downsides to having my sister remain in town permanently, it seemed. Downsides like all of my embarrassing teenage secrets no longer being secrets.

The memory did help jolt my recognition, though, and I grinned. "Angel Albright? Wow, I haven't heard of her in years."

"Of course you have! She's been in residency in Las Vegas for the last five years, but now it seems she's ready to retire!"

"And she wants to do that here?" I asked.

Gilbert nodded with pride, as if it was none other than himself who had made the celebrity want to live here.

The more I thought back to my knowledge of Angel Albright, I realised it made sense. She had always seemed to possess a childlike innocence, even as the headlines about her became more and more wild. The last thing I could remember about her was the court case where she had sued her parents for filing excessive and fraudulent expenses against her. They'd been ordered to return several millions of dollars back to her, and her father had even been sentenced to jail time.

"Well, good luck to her," I said. I'd never really bought into the celebrity machine. I believed that all people were equal, and the fact that Angel had an incredible singing voice and a bank account overflowing with money made her no better than me or anyone else in my opinion.

I thought back to Peter Rhimes, with his smart clothes and his inspection of my office. He had mentioned his client several times, but had never revealed a name, and the patient paperwork was bizarrely free from a name too.

Could Angel Albright be my new patient?

I smiled to myself. Of course, patient confidentiality meant I could reveal nothing to Gilbert about it even if she was. And chances were that someone as rich and famous as Angel would have their own dedicated physician on staff. She was hardly likely to move from a Las Vegas residency to needing to register with the local doctor's surgery.

Unless Angel was planning a low-key retirement, an attempt to live like us regular folk.

I grinned to myself. Not long ago, I had no idea that Santa was real. Now I was engaged to him and considered him and his family to be regular folk.

How strange the world is at times.

"We'll have to invite her over and welcome her to town, right? That's our job. That's... your job, Mrs Claus," Gilbert enthused.

Mrs Claus gave a quick nod. "Of course, dear. Is she moving here alone? I'd hate her to be lonely in a new place."

"Well, Yule Believe It didn't confirm that, but she does have children. Although whether she and Billie have reconciled, I really couldn't tell you," Gilbert said.

"There's no spouse?" Father Christmas asked, his

booming voice making us all jump a little as it often did. He said little and it was easy to forget he was in the room.

"No, no. She's been linked with plenty of men but has never married. She adopted three children but they're all adults now, so she could make the move here alone. Although, Angel's Angels are pretty confident she'll at least bring Gabriel."

"Angel's Angels?" I asked.

"Gabriel?" Nick asked at the same time.

Gilbert rolled his eyes at our amateur levels of knowledge, but was clearly enjoying giving us the background. "Angel's Angels, that's the community of fans. I'm on the message forum so I can say I'm an official AA, although a lot of people say they're one just by following her on Instagram. It's not really the same level of commitment, though, if you ask me."

I nodded to show my understanding. Gilbert's love of Angel Albright went deeper than I could ever have imagined.

"And Gabriel?"

"He's on staff. I guess he's her personal assistant. She never seems to go anywhere without him."

"Could he be her boyfriend?" I asked.

"That's a real entry-level conspiracy theory," Gilbert scolded me. "No, he isn't her boyfriend. He's worked for her for twenty years. At this point, he's probably one of her closest friends."

"And he's on her pay roll," Nick mumbled.

"Exactly. But he seems like a genuine guy. More genuine than her parents, in any event."

"Gilbert, this is all fascinating, but is there any chance of us eating tonight?" Father Christmas asked, and I felt my hungry stomach growl in support.

2

————

After a delicious dinner of beans on toast, Gilbert told us all that it was time he added some exercise to his daily routine, and went off into the winter wilderness.

"I don't think we need three guesses about where he's gone," August said with a wink.

"I can't believe he served us supermarket bread. I've never known him not to have a loaf freshly baked," Father Christmas muttered as he rose from his chair and left the room.

"Do you think he's going to search the streets for that singer, dear?" Mrs Claus asked. "I do worry that he's going to be disappointed. Such a fancy celebrity probably won't want to hang out here, as much as she'd be welcome."

"Is she in town already?" I asked.

"She arrived today, apparently," August confirmed with a nod of her head.

"Is she healthy?" I managed to ask, my voice weak. The image of the unfiled patient registration forms was haunting my thoughts.

August laughed. "You're hoping she joins your surgery? I'm sure she has a doctor on staff, Holly."

"I'm sure you're right," I said as I got to my feet.

The men had all left to work a late shift inspecting a new line of drones that had got the better of Father Christmas, leaving just him, me, August and Mrs Claus. Jeb was tucked up in bed asleep.

"Where are you going?" August asked.

"I need to do something. I won't be long," I said with an apologetic smile, and I bundled myself into my winter layers, ready to have another set of clothes soaked through.

"Do you fancy some company?" August asked from behind me. "I mean, if Mrs Claus wouldn't mind looking after Jeb, of course."

Mrs Claus made a simpering noise that revealed the badly kept secret of her heart - she'd been waiting a long time to have a baby to look after, and even though she hoped that baby would be her grandchild, Jeb would be a perfectly acceptable alternative for now.

"I would love nothing more," Mrs Claus said, her voice thick with emotion.

August caught my eye and we smiled at each other, then she walked back to Mrs Claus and gave the woman a kiss on her cheek.

"Thank you," I heard my sister say, and then we were away, out into the frigid evening air. A fresh snow was expected overnight, and the sky felt heavy with the barrage it would soon release.

"So, where are we off to?" August asked as we trudged through the snow already on the pavement.

"The surgery," I said.

August side-eyed me but said nothing. She knew better than to ask for information about anything patient related, but she was giving up the warmth of Claus Cottage to help me. It felt churlish to tell her nothing at all.

"I forgot to finish up some paperwork," I admitted.

"That's unlike you. Are they really so urgent?"

I nodded, and as I moved my head, a stray snowflake fell down my scarf and brushed against my neck. I shivered. "It could leave someone unable to access urgent medical care over the holidays."

"Oh," August said.

My words weren't exactly true. I would never have raced off if my doing so would leave my mystery new patient unable to access medical care. But the paperwork not being filed could certainly delay the emergency medics in accessing the patient's records, and there were plenty of treatments that couldn't be offered until those records were available. Things like whether a patient had ever had a certain vaccination, or when they'd last had a dose of a certain drug, or whether they were allergic to particular things, could all make vital differences to treatment plans.

I shook my head as I realised the kind of issues that could have been caused by my rushing out of the surgery. Sure, the worst case scenarios were unlikely, but that wasn't the same as them being impossible.

I knew better.

The High Street came into view, shop windows all ablaze with festive displays. I hadn't had time to create my own window display so August had voluntarily given up an afternoon to create the Nativity scene for me, complete with fresh hay and some of Jeb's toy animal collection. The scene was simple, obviously home-made and just perfect. It tugged on my heart strings every time I saw it.

I unlocked the door and felt grateful for the remaining warmth of the surgery.

"I won't be long," I explained as I locked the door behind us. August smiled to show me that it was fine. She was at that stage of parenting where escaping child-free for an hour was an adventure, even if all she did was trudge through the freezing snow and then sit on an industrial waiting room settee.

I grinned at her, and then turned to the reception desk.

That was when I realised that the new patient forms had gone.

3
______

"Are you sure you just left them on the desk?" August asked. She was doing her best not to scold me, but I could hear the criticism in her tone loud and clear.

Had I really left confidential papers on the desk, in plain sight, while the whole of Claus Cottage swirled with gossip about the impending arrival of an A-list celebrity?

"I can't believe I was so silly," I muttered as I rifled through the reception desk drawers.

"Don't be so hard on yourself. The surgery was locked," August said.

"That isn't the point. I should have at least put them in a drawer, out of sight."

"Holly, stop. What do you think has happened? You think someone with a key has come in here because there's an envelope on the desk?And then they've left and locked the door behind them again?"

I stopped and looked at her. "Well, what do you think has happened?"

August glanced down for a moment, then gave me an

awkward smile. "I think you've been really busy. You've had a lot going on right now, with the Christmas build-up, helping us settle in here, not to mention the engagement."

"You think I've forgotten where I put them?" I asked.

She raised an eyebrow. "It does seem like the most likely explanation, right?"

Before I could answer, there came a sudden and urgent banging at the surgery door. Grateful for the distraction from the conversation, I jumped up and unlocked the door.

And standing right there, in a baby pink sequinned gown, her hair so tousled it added at least four inches to her tiny height, was none other than Angel Albright.

"What's up, Doc?" She asked in her signature sultry voice, then took a step forward and collapsed on the surgery carpet.

"Angel? Can you hear me?" I asked as I leaned in close. Her eyes were closed, lids heavy with smoky eyeshadows and what must be a hundred coats of mascara, but her breathing was steady.

"Is she okay?" August asked.

"She's fine. Call it her secret talent," a midwestern looking man with dark hair and a flannel shirt explained as he stopped over Angel's prone figure and crossed his arms. "Gabriel Hawes, pleased to meet you."

"I'm Dr Wood. You say she's fine. How do you know?" I asked.

Gabriel shrugged a broad shoulder. He looked to be in his early 40s, and whereas everything about Angel seemed exaggerated and attention-seeking, he was a man who would blend into a scene perfectly. In fact, as I returned my gaze to Angel, I had already forgotten what he looked like.

"She doesn't always get much chance to sleep, so she

micro-naps. It's all medically supervised. I guess you've heard of Dr Piper Napperton?"

I shook my head.

"She's the best in the field. Micro-naps help circulate oxygen to the brain, and provide as much rejuvenation in three minutes as an eight-hour sleep used to."

"Used to?" August asked.

"Who has time to sleep eight hours a night now, huh?"

"Well, true," August agreed. Her own eight-hour sleeps had disappeared as soon as Jeb arrived, of course.

"You're telling me that the leading figure on naps is called Dr Napperton?" I asked.

"You're cynical. Good. That's what we need in a health-care professional. She'll be back in the room in three, two..."

Right on cue, Angel opened her famous green eyes and gave me a smile.

"Dr Wood, how lovely to meet you. Thank you for agreeing to have me as a patient."

"Ah," Gabriel reached into the back pocket of his Levis, "there was a mistake on the forms. Here you go."

"You took the forms? How?" I asked as I accepted the envelope from him.

"I have the key to the kingdom," Angel said with a seductive wink.

"But you don't have the key to my surgery," I challenged.

"She does, actually. The key to the kingdom, it's like the ultimate skeleton key. She got it with her Lifetime Contribution Award at the MegaStar Awards last year. Don't worry, we didn't look at anything else."

I was about to point out that they couldn't have because everything else was locked away, but Angel probably had a skeleton key for my filing cabinet as well.

"I'm going to input these into the system now," I said,

and unlocked the door to my own office. I fired up the computer and began to tap out the information from the forms into the patient registration software. As soon as I input the patient number on the forms, Angel's full patient file appeared on my screen.

"Do you want anything autographing?" Gabriel asked, his head poked into the doorway.

"By you?" I asked with a smile.

He grinned. "Good one! I need to get Angel to the rental cottage, but if you want anything signed, she'll do it. Could make a good Christmas present for that special someone?"

I was about to refuse, when I remembered Gilbert's adoration for the singer. "Actually, I do have someone who is a huge fan."

"Angel, get in here," Gabriel called, and in she walked. She really was tiny. And beautiful. Not to mention the star quality that seemed to radiate from her every pore. It was hard to pull my eyes away from her.

"Are you sure you don't mind? It's hardly professional, me as your doctor asking for you to sign something," I said.

She batted my concerns away with a slender hand, revealing hot pink talons. "Oh, please. I had an affair with my last doctor. The things we did in his consultation room! Ha!"

"Oh," I said as I felt my cheeks flush. "Well, I promise to treat you with more respect than that. If you're sure you're happy to, anything you feel like signing for my house elf would be hugely appreciated. He's a big fan."

"Does he want an affair with me?" Angel asked, her eyes wide.

I gaped at her, my mouth wide open.

"Knock it off," Gabriel scolded her, and she pouted like a

petulant child. Her lips looked artificially inflated, and they were shimmery with pink lipgloss.

"His name's Gilbert, and he's a very big fan of your *music*," I tried to tactfully move the subject away from any possibility of a love affair between the singer and the elf.

"I've never dated an elf before," Angel said with a wink.

"I hear Santa's quite the hunk. Maybe you should set your sights on him instead," Gabriel said as he reached into a different pocket and pulled out a postcard showing an up close photograph of Angel's face. She had a beauty spot on her cheek, bright red lipstick and eyeshadow the same shade of green as her eyes. "Here. Sign this."

"Santa's actually engaged. To me," I said, and I felt the familiar flip of my stomach as I said the words out loud.

Angel scrawled a message to Gilbert on the postcard, then looked up at me, her head cocked to one side inquisitively. "You're really engaged to Santa?"

I nodded, unsure what to expect next. Was Angel one of those celebrities who believed she was entitled to anything she set her sights on?

"That's really great," she said, and I saw a flash of the regular woman behind the make-up and the constant flirting. She gave me a smile that I knew somehow was the same smile she'd had as a child. "I love hearing about people's dreams coming true."

"Is this your dream coming true? Getting to retire and live a quieter life?" August asked from the doorway.

Angel considered the question. "I guess it is. Although Gabriel here thinks I'll be bored within a day."

Gabriel smirked. "I know you too well. You live for that stage, for that applause."

"We do have musicians here," I said. "You've heard of Michael Bauble?"

Gabriel rolled his eyes.

"I had an affair with him," Angel said with a wink. "You wouldn't believe the things we did backstage! Is he in town?"

I nodded. "He performs at most of our big events. Maybe the two of you could do a show together some time."

"Oh, I don't know..."

"Well, it's something to think about. I should probably let you both be getting home."

Angel glanced up at the clock on the wall behind my desk. "The girls should be arriving soon."

"Don't get your hopes up too much," Gabriel warned, then looked at me and grimaced. "Families, hey?"

"We all have our skeletons in the closet," I said.

"Oh, not like mine, I'm sure. Billie will hardly speak to me!" Angel exclaimed.

"She said she'd come. Let's get back and see. Cassidy and Dolly will come, you know that."

"Angel, can I say, I think it's really amazing the way you've raised your daughters away from the spotlight," August gushed.

I realised the words were true. I hadn't even realised that Angel had children until Gilbert had told me. Protecting them from the media interest couldn't have been easy.

"You're a mom?" Angel asked my sister, who nodded and beamed gratefully at the opportunity to bring the conversation to her favourite subject, her child.

"I have a baby, Jeb. Motherhood is such a rollercoaster, I can't imagine doing it with the paparazzi trailing around."

Angel gave a thoughtful smile, as if the thought hadn't occurred to her before. Of course, she had no other experience to compare it to. So much of her life, ever since she herself was a child, had been lived as a celebrity. Right from her debut as the lead in the hit movie, *Cheerleader*, she had belonged to the world.

And she had been loved, and hated, in turn ever since.

"I guess the key was making sure their attention stayed on me, not the girls," Angel said, her voice low and unsure. She was veering off script, away from the affairs and the sultry one liners, and I felt grateful to not only meet her, but to get a glimpse of the woman behind the celebrity.

"And that's something you never struggled with," Gabriel injected the lightness back into the conversation, and Angel gave a giggle.

"Where are you staying?" I asked, as I noticed that Angel's form didn't include an address.

"We have Holiday Haven rented until the New Year, then I'm going to oversee a secure compound being built over on Mistletoe Moor," Gabriel explained.

"You're worried about security?" August asked.

Angel laughed. "He's such a party pooper."

"How many kidnap attempts has it been now, Angel?" Gabriel asked.

She rolled her eyes. "Who's counting?"

"I am, and you should be too. It's been six. And they're just the ones that have been verified as a genuine threat. You've got to start taking this stuff seriously."

"But it's so dull. And I'm pretty sure there's no danger here in Candy Cane Hollow."

"You should be careful everywhere," August said.

I nodded my agreement. "Holiday Haven isn't far from us. We're at Claus Cottage. If you need anything, please stop by. Mrs Claus would love to host you for drinks."

"That's really kind," Angel said.

4

If I'd been asked to predict Gilbert's reaction to seeing the postcard autographed by Angel for him, I'd have struggled. He could have been outraged that I'd found her before him, or he could have been overjoyed, or he could have been back to his normal self and focused more on cleaning than on celebrities.

In actual fact, he took one look at the postcard and burst into tears, grabbed me for a hug and told me he loved me, then fainted.

The display of affection and emotion was out of character, and he quickly recovered from the lack of consciousness and gave me a glare that seemed to suggest I should never reveal his moment of weakness to another soul.

"Glad you like it," I said, as nonchalantly as I could.

"I guess I can find somewhere for it in my room," Gilbert said, not taking his eyes off the postcard. "Unless you need me for anything?"

"Oh, gosh, no. Go, be one with the postcard," I said with a light smile.

He eyed me, then retreated down the passage towards the kitchen, where his bedroom was just off.

August had gone straight upstairs to check on Jeb, and Mrs Claus was in her bedroom writing her speech, which would be broadcast to every home in Candy Cane Hollow on New Year's Day.

I decided to sit in the den and enjoy some quiet for a while, but no sooner had I taken a seat than the doorbell rang. I listened out for the usual sound of Gilbert's scuttle of feet, but heard none, and got up myself. I wasn't against answering the door, I had just learned that Gilbert took offence whenever another person beat him to the job.

I even checked the hallway, but the coast was clear. He must have been very distracted by the Angel postcard.

I opened the door and a small, bald-headed man in a long, camel coat and designer striped scarf grinned at me.

"Good evening," I said, hoping my voice was friendly despite the fact that I had no idea who the unexpected caller was.

"You must be Holly Wood, newly engaged to Santa. Festive greetings to you!"

"And to you, Mr…"

"Berevit," he said with another winning smile. "Yule Berevit."

"Oh! You run the gossip…"

"The online news column. Yes, yes, one and the same. Could I trouble you to come in for a moment? It's for a very important story."

"Erm. I mean, yes, of course you can come in. We don't comment on news stories, though," I explained. Mrs Claus was impartial, like the Queen, Santa rest her soul.

"Of course, of course. I understand you've had a

personal meet and greet with Candy Cane Hollow's latest A-list resident?"

I gazed at the man with my brow furrowed. "I couldn't possibly..."

"Confirm or deny. Sure, I understand. Dreadfully restrictive duty of confidentiality, isn't it? Could I trouble you for a hot chocolate, by the way?"

"Erm, sure," I agreed. I couldn't dare risk Gilbert's reputation by proxy by refusing the man, even if I was incredibly uncomfortable with the idea of a journalist being in Claus Cottage.

I left Yule alone in the den and hastily made my way down the passage, past the kitchen, to Gilbert's quarters. I'd never been in the elf's bedroom before and wasn't sure how welcome I'd be in his sacred space. I rapped on the door lightly.

To my surprise, Gilbert didn't open the door, but peered at me through a peep hole built into the wood.

"What do you need?" He asked.

"We have a visitor. And they want hot chocolate," I whispered.

"Why didn't you say! I'll be right out!" Gilbert exclaimed, then shut the peep hole. I heard scuffling around in the room and left him to it, making my way to the kitchen, where I filled the kettle with water and selected a cup for our guest.

Gilbert emerged behind me within just a moment or two, his complexion a little more orange than normal. And was he wearing false eyelashes?

"Are you okay?" I asked.

"Fine. What on earth are you doing?" He asked, his beady eyes focused on the kettle. As he stomped past me and switched the thing off, I saw a distinctively unblended line of orange around his chin.

"Are you wearing make-up?" I asked.

"Are you making a hot chocolate with water?" He challenged me, as he pulled the whole milk from the fridge and measured out enough to make a full round of his signature drink.

"I forgot the Golden Rule, sorry," I admitted. I made hot chocolates so rarely, when I did attempt it, it was easy to slip back into the way I'd been brought up to make them - with hot water and not a bit of milk.

Only since I'd arrived in Candy Cane Hollow had I realised that the making of a hot chocolate was considered a fine art, and nobody did it better than Gilbert.

"Why don't I make these and you go ahead and chat to Mr Berevit?" I offered.

Gilbert eyeballed me, and I thought there was a slight flick of mascara on his eyelashes. "What are you saying, Holly? Am I suddenly incapable of running this kitchen? Do you want my job?"

"Erm, no, definitely not," I protested.

"I've got a good mind to hang up my apron strings and call it a day! Hold on, did you say Mr Berevit?"

I stifled a laugh. "Yule Berevit, from the column you like. He's here about a story he's writing."

"Well, goodness. Is it really him? There are impersonators, you know. They claim to be him in the hopes of getting information or freebies. Is it really him, Holly?"

"Well, I didn't ask to see the man's ID," I admitted. "He does look very distinctive, though."

"Yes, he does. I'll finish these drinks and come right out."

"I'll wait with you," I said. "And, Gilbert, if you do have make-up on, it might need blending a little more."

The elf paused his gentle whisking of the milk as it

warmed in a pan, and assessed me. I wasn't making fun of him. I didn't care whether he wore a full face of make-up or none at all. It wasn't my business.

He rolled his eyes and flashed me a smile. "I was taking a selfie with the Angel postcard, you know, to send to family, and I thought I should look my best for it."

Dressing up for a postcard. I'd heard everything now. "You always look your best, Gilbert. And we love you exactly as you are."

The elf pursed his lips, back to his normal self uncomfortable around affection, and finished off the hot chocolates. He carried the tray of drinks but allowed me to open the den door, where Yule Berevit stood, his back to us, a phone clasped to his ear.

"It goes to press. I don't care when you think you should have finished work for the day. News never stops! Send it live now, or you'll have no job to return to in the new year."

Gilbert and I shared an ominous glance as Yule spun around and gave us a long-suffering smile.

"Interns. They promise the earth and turn out to be useless. Now, I'm glad you could meet with me, Dr Wood."

Gilbert stood next to me, his eyes fixed on the reporter he so admired.

"This is Gilbert, our house elf. He's the finest in Candy Cane Hollow," I introduced.

Gilbert held out a hand, but Yule only looked at it with an air of distaste, and lowered himself into one of the seats.

"I'm not sure this is a conversation for the staff, Dr Wood," Yule said.

I gasped. "Gilbert is part of the family. Whatever you want to say to me, he can hear. Although, as I've already said, we don't comment on news stories."

"Yes, yes, I've heard. I'm here to tell you something that

may interest you. Angel is in town. Don't look surprised. I know you've seen her."

"How do you know that?" I asked. If he was telling the truth, someone must have shared the details of our meeting with him. Who would have done such a thing, and so quickly?

"It's my job to know everything. Did she tell you about the kidnap attempt?"

"I can't comment on anything," I repeated. Yule Berevit was starting to bug me.

"There's been another one?" Gilbert asked, his eyes wide. He was definitely wearing mascara.

"Ah, you follow the news?"

"I never miss an article," Gilbert shared with pride.

"It's good to meet someone with fine taste. And yes, to answer your question, there's another kidnap attempt being planned."

Gilbert gasped.

I rolled my eyes. It seemed clear to me that Yule Berevit was a sensationalist. "If that's true, shouldn't you be speaking to the police about it? Or warning Angel?"

Yule raised a perfectly sculpted eyebrow in my direction. "You really don't follow the news, do you? Quite disappointing in a professional like yourself, Dr Wood. Angel hasn't spoken to the press in nearly a decade."

"I'm sure a message about her safety would reach her somehow, if you were determined," I said.

Yule smiled the smile of a lazy cat who had just had a second serving of cream. "Here I am, doing exactly that."

"We can get a message to her," Gilbert said. He was sitting so far forward in the chair that he was almost on the floor.

"Excellent. And in return, all I'll need is a quote about Angel relocating to Candy Cane Hollow."

"You're blackmailing us?" I asked.

"I'm not sure that's the word for it. It's a business deal. We all have to make a living, Dr Wood. My currency is exclusives."

"I have nothing to tell you," I insisted.

"That's a shame. And you, Mr Elf, do you have a quote for me? I can put your name in lights all over YuleBelieve It.com!"

I glanced at Gilbert and silently urged him to make the right decision. He glanced at me, gave me an apologetic smile, then sat back in his chair and met Yule's gaze.

"The residents of Claus Cottage do not comment on the news. We are impartial," Gilbert said, taking care to pronounce each word. Then, he rose from his chair. "Mr Berevit, I believe I should show you out now."

And with that, I watched in stunned silence as Gilbert kicked out a guest.

5

—————

As soon as Yule Berevit was off the premises, I called Wiggles. The leader of Candy Cane Hollow's police force was an easy man to underestimate, what with his love of Wham!'s Last Christmas, his surprisingly glittery wardrobe, and his jolly demeanour.

His phone wasn't answered by him, though, but by another voice I recognised.

"Cornelius?" I asked.

"Ah! Dr Wood, good tidings to you!" Cornelius barked into the phone. Wiggles' old friend looked like a walrus, and had the personality to match.

"I didn't realise you were in town," I said. I'd only met Cornelius recently, but he had made an impression on me right away. I suspected he made an impression on everyone he met.

"I had to come back and share some intel with Wiggles. Did you know Angel Albright has made this place her new home?"

I disguised a laugh. "Yes, I've heard that rumour."

"It's more than a rumour, lassie. She's here, and her life is in grave danger."

"The kidnap plan, you mean?"

Cornelius scoffed. "You know about it too?"

"I've just had a visit from Yule Berevit. He mentioned the kidnap plans but wouldn't share any more than that. I wanted to make sure Wiggles was aware."

"Good lass. Yes, yes, he's on it. You hear all sorts on the pirate radio station, let me tell you. One time, back in '74 it must have been, there was a rumour that evil clowns were going to take over the world. That ruffled a few feathers, I can tell you. Turned out to be a false alarm, which I'll admit seems pretty obvious now. But at the time, ooh let me tell you, it was a scary time to be alive."

"It sounds it," I agreed.

A noise from the hallway distracted me and I looked across to see Gilbert stepping into his Wellington boots.

"What are you doing?" I asked.

"We're just driving around, lassie, making sure there are no suspicious characters out and about. Don't you worry, we'll make sure that Angel stays safe," Cornelius said, thinking I was speaking to him.

"I'm going out there. I need to protect Angel," Gilbert explained as he grabbed his heavy duffel coat and slipped it on.

I groaned. The promise of a quiet, relaxed evening was quickly disappearing from my future.

"Cornelius, can we come with you? Gilbert and I would like to help," I said.

"Yes, yes! Let's get this thing up to Claus Cottage, pronto! We'll see you in a jiffy, lassie," Cornelius said, before ending the call.

Gilbert stood in the doorway, poised ready to leave.

"Are you sure about this, Gilbert? It could be dangerous out there," I asked.

"I laugh in the face of danger," the elf said, before attempting an evil cackle that ended with him descending into a wild coughing fit.

Light footsteps treaded their way downstairs, and I turned to see August looking at me quizzically. "Going somewhere?"

"We won't be long. I hope," I explained and planted a kiss on her cheek.

"Okay. Don't do anything silly," she said. "You have that glint in your eye that you used to get when you were attempting to run a DIY version of the Krypton Factor."

I laughed. I hadn't thought of that physical activity game show in years. "It really is good to have you here, sis."

The tinny tune of Last Christmas became audible and Gilbert and I nodded at each other.

"Let's do this," we murmured, and we dashed out of Claus Cottage and met Wiggles' tiny Fiat as it struggled up the hill. Squeezing into the back seat was no easy feat, but we somehow managed it.

"Where's Angel staying?" Wiggles asked me by way of hello, once I had got into place and fastened my seatbelt.

"Her assistant mentioned some place called Holiday Haven," I said, the name of the rental home returning to me.

"I know it. All of the VIPs stay there," Wiggles said as he began to drive. The streets were calm and quiet, and a fresh snowfall had just began. Snowflakes floated down from the sky at a leisurely pace, none of them appearing to be in a rush.

It only took thirteen and a half renditions of Last Christmas for us to see the warm glow of lights up ahead. Holiday Haven really was a haven, nestled into the permanently decorated and lit foliage of the Festive Forest. It was a large, modern building with a front that was almost entirely glass.

Cornelius let out an ear-piercing whistle. "That place must cost a pretty penny to rent out."

"I can't imagine Angel Albright has to worry about such things," Wiggles said with a chuckle as he parked the car and turned off the headlights.

"I see her!" Gilbert exclaimed, his nose practically glued to the car window.

I followed his gaze and saw that he was right. Angel Albright, dressed in a fur lined negligee, her blond hair piled up on top of her head, was standing in the kitchen, appearing to concentrate on something on the work surface.

"Is she cooking?" I asked, as I spotted the glint of the sharp knife in her hand. The image was bizarre; the world's most sultry celebrity, spending a quiet evening at home.

"She's vegan," Gilbert said, which wasn't really an answer but an opportunity for him to reveal how much he knew about her.

"I'm pretty sure I saw a photo of her eating a burger just a few weeks ago," Cornelius said with a wink.

Gilbert shook his head. "She's always being set up like that. The press keep trying to drag her down. If she was eating a burger, it would have been vegan, I can assure you of that."

Cornelius turned to me and grinned.

"I wonder if she's lonely," I murmured.

Before anyone could interrupt, there came a knock on Wiggles' window and all of us inside the vehicle jumped, which made the tiny car itself do a jump as well.

Glaring in at us was a young woman with pixie-like ears, long dark hair and a furious scowl.

"Oh-em-gee, it's Cassidy!" Gilbert squealed. At my blank look, he handily filled in the silence. "Middle daughter. Twenty years old."

Wiggles wound down the window by hand and a flurry of snow shot into the vehicle, hitting our faces.

"Wow, is this the new 'Fiat Stakeout' model? I didn't realise Candy Cane Hollow had its very own secret spy agency! Are you guys on a mission to save Christmas cookies from disappearing or something?" Cassidy drawled. Her accent was a confused blend that I imagined reflected her wide travel as a child.

Gilbert broke out into crazed laughter. "Man, you really are as funny as legend says!"

"Who are you and what are you doing here?" The young woman asked, her arms crossed, as any good humour disappeared from her.

Wiggles held out his police badge. "We're here to ensure Ms Albright remains safe."

Cassidy rolled her eyes. "You'd better come inside then instead of skulking around out here. Come on, you're just in time for her famous cheese board."

Cornelius raised a bushy eyebrow at Gilbert, who gave a nervous laugh. "Vegan, I'm sure."

We all trudged out of the car and through the snow.

As I stepped through the grand entrance of Angel's luxurious holiday rental, a sense of wonder enveloped me. The spacious interior seemed to merge seamlessly with the snowy landscape beyond, thanks to the expansive glass windows that framed breathtaking views of the winter wonderland. The open-concept design brought a feeling of grandeur, while the modern fireplace crackled warmly, its flames dancing in harmony with the glistening snowflakes outside. My gaze was drawn to sleek furnishings that invited relaxation, their plush cushions seemingly an invitation to unwind. Every corner was adorned with tasteful holiday decorations, twinkling lights casting a cozy glow over the sleek surfaces and modern amenities. The scent of evergreens and the soft hum of contemporary appliances combined, creating an ambiance that merged the enchantment of the season with the comfort of the present day.

Angel smiled at us and opened the huge fridge, pulling out a glass of Champagne, which all of us apart from Gilbert demurely refused.

"Ms Albright, it is the greatest honour," he said, as he accepted the glass from her.

"Oh, no, the honour is all mine. It's so good to meet my new neighbours," Angel gushed.

"Mama, these people are apparently here to check you're safe," Cassidy said. She eyed us warily. I wondered what it must have been like for her, growing up as a daughter of such a huge celebrity.

"Well, I am! Ta da!" Angel said, and did a twirl. I realised that she was wearing glass high-heeled stilettos, like Cinderella. Inside her own house. I could barely get through a formal meeting in heels without my feet burning with pain.

"Ma'am, we have reports of a kidnapping plan against you. We have reason to take it as a serious threat," Wiggles explained.

Angel bit her lip and then giggled. "Oh, look at you! So strong and protective! I really do appreciate it, sheriff."

Wiggles didn't correct her. She wasn't in the USA any longer, and we didn't have sheriffs.

"But I refuse to stop living my life the way I want to, just because of a couple of crazy people with silly ideas!"

"These aren't crazy people. I heard them with my own ears," Cornelius interjected.

"You did?" Angel asked, her eyes wide.

Cornelius nodded, and so did his jowls. "I'm something of a ham radio connoisseur, you see. CWLRS is my code name, don't go sharing that with anyone. I listen to the pirate radio to keep abreast of the news. By the time anything makes its way to regular broadcasting, it's too late."

"And you heard what, exactly? Did these people really build a kidnapping plot over a radio channel?" Cassidy asked.

"They did indeed, lassie."

"And they're going to take me tonight?" Angel asked.

Cornelius looked at her blankly.

"You've come out here to stop it happening, right? So it's going to be tonight?" Cassidy asked, clearly following her mother's line of thinking.

"Well, I don't know when exactly," Cornelius admitted.

"But they'll be taking mama from here? They know where she's staying?" Cassidy pushed.

"Is dinner nearly ready? I have to get back to studying in six minutes," a voice came, and we all turned to see another young lady, this one dark-skinned with a full Afro, enter the kitchen.

"We have company, Dolly," Angel said with a smile.

"The youngest daughter," Gilbert whispered by my side. "She's going to be a lawyer. She already divides her days into six minute blocks because that's how lawyers bill clients."

"Oh. Great. We came all the way here to get rid of people, and we don't last more than 42 minutes without company."

"Actually, will you join us for dinner? It's only cheese

and biscuits, I'm afraid. Dolly does need to eat though. She can't disrupt her study schedule," Angel explained.

We all took seats around the large kitchen island, and watched as Angel brought masses of food out to us. What she called humble cheese and biscuits turned out to be the most extravagant charcuterie board I had ever seen in my life.

"She loves to host," Gilbert whispered. His constant narration of the evening's activities was sweet, and I gripped his hand and gave it a squeeze. The glass of champagne was still firmly gripped in his other hand and I suspected he'd be attempting to sneak it out with him and save it as a souvenir.

"Eat, please! You came out here in this weather, and I'm very grateful, even if it was unnecessary," Angel said with a smile. I was sure she had topped up her lip gloss since we arrived, and yet she hadn't left the room. Did celebrities get magical powers?

"They think mama's going to be kidnapped," Cassidy explained to her younger sister.

"Again?" Dolly asked as she loaded a cracker with foie gras.

"I've never actually been kidnapped, girls, and I'm not about to start now. Not just as I try to settle down and enjoy a quiet life!"

"What intel exactly are you acting on?" Cassidy asked, squaring her gaze at Cornelius.

"Well, as I was saying, I came across the plot being finalised, but everything is in code. What I can tell you for sure is that this plan has taken considerable time to finalise. The kidnapper has been building resources for some time, and they plan to take your mother prisoner," Cornelius explained as he took a bite of a bruschetta topped generously with crumbly cheese, which broke off and promptly hid in his beard.

"And you don't know who this mystery person is?" Cassidy asked.

"They go by Mr X," Cornelius said.

"Ugh, Mr X. That's not even creative," Cassidy said with a groan.

"So it's a woman," Dolly said.

"Not necessarily," Cassidy argued.

"It's pretty obvious that the inclusion of a gender moniker is only done as a red herring. Our kidnapper is a woman, I can assure you," Dolly said. She had loaded her own plate with an incredible amount of food for someone with such a tiny frame, but she did look like a teenager. And the food was delicious.

"Maybe it's you," Cassidy teased.

"Maybe it's Billie," Dolly deadpanned.

"The prodigal daughter," Gilbert whispered in my ear. I didn't point out that she wasn't prodigal until she returned.

"Hush now, girls, we don't gossip and we don't speak about people who aren't here," Angel chastised them. To my impressed surprise, the girls said nothing more and we all ate in a companionable silence for a few moments.

"Angel, do you and the girls have plans tomorrow?" I asked.

"We'll be attending our local church's service, by video link of course. Then we're going to have a family Christmas. I'll cook a full dinner."

"You'd be welcome to join us over at Claus Cottage for the day, if you'd like," I offered. I felt sure that Mrs Claus would extend the invitation if she was here. She'd hate to imagine that newcomers to Candy Cane Hollow hadn't been treated hospitably.

"Oh, that's really sweet of you. Thank you."

"Christmas Day is a family day though," Cassidy said with a smile.

"That's right. I spend it with my girls every year. Just the four of us," Angel said with a grin.

"Just the three of us this year," Dolly corrected.

"There's still time for Billie to arrive," Angel said. "You know what she's like."

"She's the problem child," Cassidy deadpanned as she looked right at me.

"Now, now," Angel said.

"I think most of us had our difficult patches as we grew up. I'm sure she'll be here if she can," I offered.

"Difficult patch? Ha! She's writing a memoir, you know?" Cassidy said.

Gilbert gasped beside me. Clearly that news wasn't well-known.

"It's her right to explore her lived experience. My therapist says it's a positive sign," Angel said, her smile not quite reaching her eyes.

"Angel's Villain is the working title. Can you believe that? She's using her own mother as a cash cow. Not that she needs the money. She just wants the attention," Cassidy said.

"Of course she does. She has a very demonstrative personality. It can't be easy for any of you girls, being raised in this bubble," Angel said. Seeing her switch from A-list celebrity to regular mother was fascinating. The woman was more multi-faceted than I had ever imagined.

"It has its upsides," Cassidy said, and she leaned over and kissed her mother on the cheek. Angel's eyes glinted with pleasure.

"Ms Albright, I'm sorry for being the party pooper here,

but I think spending tomorrow away from this address would be a wise idea," Wiggles interjected.

"Nonsense. Nobody knows I'm staying here. We're perfectly safe," Angel insisted.

"Holiday Haven is the most luxurious rental. It's the obvious choice for your location," Wiggles argued.

"Officer, I appreciate the concern, but I'm not uprooting my daughters. This is our home for this Christmas. We have all of our decorations ready. We have a turkey already thawing. I will not leave."

"I really have to insist," Wiggles said, his tone firmer than I had ever heard before.

"This is the address Billie has," Dolly murmured, her voice barely more than a whisper.

We all sat in silence for a few moments as we realised the true reason Angel wouldn't relocate. She was nothing more than a hopeful mother, praying her estranged daughter returned to her. Their reunion was probably on her Christmas list, alongside the latest Chanel perfume and a thoroughbred horse... or whatever A-list celebrities enjoyed owning.

"Could we get a message to her for you? I'm sure she'd be welcome at Claus Cottage," Cornelius suggested.

I nodded my agreement. Mrs Claus had an inability to refuse any waifs and strays; that was how I had ended up finding myself in Candy Cane Hollow. And while Gilbert may ordinarily be put out by the addition of another guest for dinner, he would love nothing more than cooking for Angel Albright.

"She's blocked us," Cassidy said with an eye roll. Despite her being younger than Billie, she clearly thought her sister's behaviour was childish.

"She hasn't blocked me," Dolly admitted, her cheeks red.

"Dolores Margaret Albright, what on earth did you just say?" Angel asked, all of her attention focused on her youngest child.

Dolly gazed down at her plate, unable to meet her mother's gaze. "I didn't realise until a few days ago. I sent her a Merry Christmas text and it was delivered."

"And?" Angel asked.

Dolly shrugged. "She hasn't replied. But I went on her Instagram afterwards and I could see her account."

"Show me," Angel urged. If she felt any awkwardness about this family drama playing out with guests around the table, she didn't show it. There was clearly nothing more important to her than her daughters, and I found the whole scene heartbreaking and touching all at the same time.

If Angel Albright could be racked with turmoil over the state of her relationship with her children, what hope did any of us mere mortals have for surviving motherhood without our hearts being pummelled like PlayDoh?

Not that I was thinking about having a baby. Gosh, if Mrs Claus could read my mind she'd already be knitting baby hats.

Dolly obediently pulled her phone out of her jeans pocket and tapped the screen a few times, then laid it out on the table in front of Angel, who scrolled and gasped.

"She's in Dubai?" Angel asked.

"With Lil Bo Cheep?" Cassidy asked, her nose turned up in disgust.

"Who?" Wiggles asked.

"Lil Bo Cheep, you know him, surely? He's an up and coming rapper. Best known for Cheep Cheep Bo, although I prefer the cool melody of Cheep It Real," Cornelius explained.

We all looked at him in stunned silence for a moment.

"Is he a good guy?" Angel asked him, and it was hard to remember that she was a celebrity. All of her usual glitter and star magic had disappeared, and she looked for all of the world like a concerned mum, a rather sad figure who had prepared a meal she could barely eat, and was picking at it in a negligee and glass slippers, no doubt just in case the paparazzi were outside.

"Well, I've only met him once," Cornelius explained.

"*You* have met Lil Bo Cheep?" Cassidy asked incredulously.

Cornelius nodded. "I don't want to say I discovered him, but I was there for his first gig. I like to surf the small venues. It's a wonderful way to spot the next big thing. I offered Cheep a few tips about some of his rhymes, that's all."

"You gave him rhyme advice?"

Cornelius shrugged. "I don't want to speak out of school, but he was being a little too generous with what counted as a rhyme. He's tightened it all up now."

"But was he a good guy?" Angel pleaded, her eyes wide.

"Oh yes! A real sweetheart," Cornelius said with a grin.

We were interrupted by a firm knock at the door. Angel jumped as if she had been struck by lightning, but Wiggles was up on his feet before her.

"Allow me. You all stay in here," he insisted.

We heard muffled voices after he had answered the front door, and all of us sat in a hushed silence so we could each attempt to figure out who was there.

After a few moments, Wiggles returned to the room, a man and woman behind him. I judged by Gilbert's gasp that the new guests were Billie and Lil Bo Cheep.

Billie was tall, easily over six feet, and was covered in tattoos. Her bright red hair was piled on top of her head like a beehive, and instead of glamorous heels like her mother's, she was wearing heavy combat boots.

Lil Bo Cheep had hair in dreads, a plaster on his cheek, and a teardrop tattoo that I understood to mean he was claiming to have taken one person's life. He had a boyish smile, though, and while Billie appeared hostile, he seemed almost nervous to be here.

"Angel, I'm a big fan," he broke the silence and crossed the room to shake her hand.

"Well, thank you. It was nice of you to accompany Billie home, but I'm sure she's told you we have a family only policy for Christmas," Angel said.

Cheep gave a lopsided smile. "Oh, erm, I…"

"He is family, mother," Billie said, her hands still tucked in her pockets. Despite being the oldest child, already 22 years old, she acted like the youngest with her scowling face and harsh tone.

"I'm sure he's a very nice gentleman. In fact, one of our guests was just telling us what a nice person he considers Cheep to be," Angel said.

Cornelius gave a little wave and to my surprise, Cheep lit up with recognition immediately.

"Yo, Big C in da house!"

Cornelius' cheeks flushed.

"He really does know him," Gilbert voiced what everyone was thinking.

"You're welcome to stay for a drink, but then I must ask…" Angel began.

"We're married, mother," Billie revealed, and finally pulled her hands from her pockets, to reveal a modest ring with a black stone in the centre.

There was no time to respond to that revelation because

there came another knock at the door, this one panicked and thunderous.

We all filed out to the lobby and Wiggles opened the door to reveal Gabriel stood before us, his flannel shirt soaked through with blood.

6

We got Gabriel indoors, locked the door and sat him on an expensive looking settee that would no doubt be ruined. Angel wouldn't be getting her security deposit back for this rental, that was for sure.

It took Gabriel a few minutes and a cup of brandy before his ragged breathing calmed a little and he appeared able to focus on where he was.

A quick examination had shown me that he was not injured, which left us with the disconcerting realisation that the blood was someone else's.

"Now, take a breath and tell us everything you remember," Wiggles instructed.

Gabriel said nothing, but turned in his seat and looked out into the night. It was impossible to see anything out there. With the lights on indoors, all the window showed was a reflection of us. Our faces were all etched with worry.

"I think he's telling us it's out there," Cornelius said.

"We'll go and investigate. The rest of you stay here," Wiggles commanded.

"I'm coming," I said.

Wiggles appeared to have no energy left to argue, so he led the way and the three of us moved as if in a snake formation, out of the house and into the frigid evening air.

The snow had been falling all afternoon and continued, giving the outdoors a winter wonderland look but with a sinister feel. Snow was great for hiding tracks, hiding evidence, even hiding bodies.

We didn't get far before Wiggles put up a hand, and I stopped moving forward. There was a lump half-hidden in the snow, which had a pinkish tinge.

I felt my stomach sink as I realised the lump was human-sized. Wiggles managed to get the snow moved enough to reveal a person's face. I looked away like a coward. The truth was, that charcuterie board was full of beautiful rich food and I was worried I might be a little more prone to vomiting than I normally would have been.

"Anyone recognise this poor fellow?" Wiggles asked.

I forced myself to take a look. The skin tone alone made it clear that my medical training wouldn't be necessary.

"Never seen him before," Cornelius admitted.

I moved in closer and gasped. "That's Mr Rhimes. He's Angel's lawyer. Or, at least, he was."

Wiggles frowned. "I wonder what he was doing out here. Angel made it clear Christmas is just for family."

"Maybe she considers him to be family," Cornelius suggested.

I shook my head. "I doubt it. Their relationship seemed professional to me."

"Well, let's get back in there and break the news," Wiggles said. None of us noticed as we turned that the house was in darkness. It wasn't until we pushed open the front door that we realised the lights had gone out.

"What the heck..." Wiggles muttered.

"Are you okay in there?" Cornelius called through.

"Yes," came the jumbled reply of several voices.

"I'll handle this. I'm something of an expert when it comes to power outages," Cornelius volunteered.

"You are?"

Cornelius gave an enthusiastic nod. "It's either hire qualified workmen when you drill through a wire, or learn how to sort it out yourself. I'm a quick learner. I'll be back in a jiffy."

"Just stay put in there! We'll have the lights on in a second," Wiggles called through. A general murmur, unhappy but accepting of the advice, came back in reply.

"So," Wiggles said. "You knew that poor guy out in the snow?"

I nodded, not that Wiggles could see. I could barely make out his outline in the darkness. "He came to me to set up Angel as a new patient."

"What did you make of him?"

I shrugged. "He seemed very formal. Old school. He was in a full suit, even in the snow. He quizzed me about my security and confidentiality before leaving Angel's details with me."

"Hmm. I guess Angel's the best person to give us details about him."

"I'd imagine so," I agreed. Angel seemed to build long relationships with her staff.

All of a sudden, the lights went on and a cheer came from the other room. Cornelius was back with us, a grin on his face as he waggled his eyebrows.

"You did it!" I exclaimed, my voice revealing more surprise than was helpful.

"There's a few tricks in the old dog yet," he said with a

wink. Thankfully, Cornelius had tough skin. It was hard to offend him.

Wiggles pushed open the door and we rejoined the others, who looked anguished from the darkness.

"Hold on, where's mama?" Cassidy asked.

Everyone glanced at each other, but her observation was correct. Angel was no longer in the room.

"She probably went to try and sort out the power. You know she has to wade into every mess and make it worse," Billie said with an eye roll.

"That's not fair. All she's ever done is take care of us all! Not that you've ever said thank you," Dolly argued, her eyes fierce and harsh.

"You're such a baby, Dolly. You don't know anything about life yet. Grow up a bit and then we can talk," Billie said as she draped herself into Cheep's arms.

"Did anyone hear Angel leave?" Wiggles asked. Everyone looked at each other.

"There was some scuffling around. I think someone moved around and banged into something," Cheep offered.

"But Angel didn't say she was going to check the lights?" I asked.

Cassidy shook her head and met my gaze. "It's the kidnap attempt, isn't it? Someone's taken her! They switched off the power and then took her!"

"We have to find her," Dolly said, and the two of them linked arms and headed towards the front of the house.

"Not so fast," Wiggles objected.

"You can't stop us!" Cassidy argued.

"Actually, I can. And you definitely don't want to go out that way."

"Why not? What aren't you telling us?" Dolly asked.

Wiggles glanced at me and opened his mouth, but

before he could say a word, Cornelius beat him to it, with all of his usual discretion and tact.

"Your mother's lawyer is out there. He's been killed and someone has dumped his dead body out in the snow."

That was when the tough guy of r'n'b, Lil Bo Cheep, fainted.

He came around surprisingly fast and blushed when he saw the look of disdain that Billie had for him.

"I didn't realise I'd married a wimp," she said with one eyebrow raised as her sisters helped her husband into a chair.

"That's what happens when you marry a virtual stranger, sis," Cassidy quipped.

"Listen, we need to stay focused. We're all going to stay right here until your mother is found, not least because the outside of this place is a crime scene. I'll call the station and get some officers out here to check for evidence," Wiggles said.

"And what are we meant to do while our mother is off gallivanting with a deranged fan?" Billie asked.

"Billie! She's been kidnapped! She's in grave danger!" Cassidy exclaimed.

Billie rolled her eyes. "*She* never took those threats seriously before. Why should *I* now? She just wants to upstage me yet again."

"What on earth are you talking about?"

"The biggest news to hit the papers tomorrow was going to be me getting married! But, oh no! Angel Albright has to go and get herself kidnapped. That's my story pushed all the way back to the middle pages... yet again."

Dolly shook her head. "You really are unbelievable. Officer, what can I do to help? I have mama's phone stored in Find My Friends. Shall we check that?"

"Great idea!" Cornelius barked. He was always enthusiastic when technology was involved.

"I'll just fetch my phone from my bedroom," Dolly said.

"I'll go with you," I said. "It's best that nobody is alone right now."

Dolly nodded, and we left the main room together and made our way upstairs. Dolly's room had a large desk and her laptop was open on it. It had set itself into sleep mode as she had been away much longer than her planned six minute study break.

Her phone had been tossed carelessly on her bed, and she grabbed it, tapped away at the screen, then groaned.

"What is it?" I asked.

She held the phone up and I saw the flashing icon that indicated the location of Angel's phone.

"It's in the garden," Dolly whispered.

My heart sank, but I forced a smile to my face. "That doesn't necessarily mean anything. Let's go back downstairs and show Wiggles. He'll have a plan."

Dolly nodded. "I can't believe this is happening."

"I know."

"No, I mean I can't believe it's happening now. I've shared her with the world for my whole life, and finally it was going to be just us. No more dramas. No more touring. No more paparazzi. I just... I really wanted this to work out."

I opened my arms and allowed Dolly to fall into them. Her tiny body began to shake as she cried to me.

If this didn't get sorted, the world would have lost an icon, but Dolly would have lost her mother.

"We'll find her," I whispered.

"You promise?"

"Of course," I said. I could promise no such thing, but I was incapable of any other reply.

7

____

It was decided that Wiggles and Cornelius would search the garden for the phone, and I would keep check that everyone else remained in the great room.

The last thing we needed was another person disappearing.

The minutes dragged on in awkward silence until there was a ping of a notification, and Cassidy pulled her mobile phone from her pocket. She looked at the screen and groaned.

"What is it?" Dolly asked.

"The story's out," Cassidy said.

"The wedding?" Billie asked hopefully.

Cassidy rolled her eyes. "No, not the wedding, you moron. There's only one story here and it's that our mother has been kidnapped!"

"My life has never mattered to you, has it?" Billie flew up out of her seat in a rage and glared at her sister. Cheep pulled on her arm and she fought her way out of his reach, slapping him across the face with the back of her hand as she did so. He blinked up at her in a dazed confusion, but said nothing.

It was a revelation to me that the r'n'b bad boy was so mild-mannered.

"What does it say?" Dolly asked, her voice barely a whisper. "Is it a ransom demand?"

Cassidy scanned the article on her phone and shook her head. "THE DEVIL SNARES ANGEL is the headline. A source close to pop legend Angel Albright has confirmed that the singer, 42, has been kidnapped. Kidnap threats have plagued the star, who shot to fame when she was just 15, and she is renowned for refusing to take such threats seriously. The celebrity mum of three has recently retired from her Las Vegas residency, which was the longest-running and most popular in residency history. She planned to focus on quality time with her family. Let's hope she's returned safely so her Christmas wish can be granted."

"A source close to her. I wonder who that was?" I said, not even realising I had asked the question out loud.

"Well, you know for sure it wasn't me. I was in no urgency for this news to break!" Billie said with a scowl. Cheep reached across and took her hand in his. Every finger had two tattoos on; tiny images of crowns, music notes, letters. The man was like a human colouring book.

"Maybe it's good that word is out fast," Dolly said hopefully.

Cassidy frowned. "Every attention seeker and deranged fan is going to be making calls now, pretending they've got her. We'll never figure out whether any of them are genuine."

"Well, that won't be your job. The police will take care of everything," I said.

Gabriel came out of his shocked stupor enough to give a crazed cackle. "What have the police ever done for Angel?"

"What do you mean?" I asked.

He batted a hand at me. "Never mind. Forget it. You're obviously a police sympathiser."

"I don't even know what that means," I said.

"Exactly," he spat.

The whole conversation felt like I was trying to win a tickling match against a caterpillar, so I said nothing else.

Thankfully, I was rescued from any further attempts to speak to the group. Cornelius and Wiggles returned, and Wiggles held a phone up in his hand.

"Is this Angel's?"

Dolly glanced across and nodded. It was a surprisingly old model of a popular brand, and I thought again that Angel had more depth to her than the newspapers would like us to believe.

"There are faint footprints out there. It's hard to make out as there's fresh snow covering them already, but I think it's fair to assume that Angel was kidnapped," Wiggles announced.

"Really, Mr Cop? Is that your amazing scoop? 'Breaking news: Water is wet and the sky is up!' Maybe next you'll tell us the sun rises in the east!" Cassidy quipped.

Wiggles glanced at me.

"It's all over the news already," I revealed through gritted teeth.

Wiggles raised an eyebrow. "Is there a ransom?"

I shook my head. "A source close to Angel has called it in."

Wiggles gave a slow nod and scanned the room, his eyes flicking suspiciously from one person to the next.

"I've already said it's not me!" Billie exclaimed when Wiggles looked her way.

"Sometimes the guilty people really do protest too much," Cassidy muttered.

Cheep reached out and pulled Billie in to his arms. "It's okay, babe."

Cassidy crinkled her nose in disgust at his affection.

"What have you got against Cheep? You barely know him!"

Cassidy laughed. "We have something in common for once."

"Can you guys cut this out. We have to focus on finding mama, and if somebody's already contacted the press, that's probably one of us. Right?"

Wiggles considered the question, but thankfully Cornelius steamrolled over him with his usual tact.

"It's most likely someone in this room. Anyone want to confess?"

"Is it a crime to speak to a journalist now?" Billie asked.

Cassidy laughed. "It's not even a journalist. It's whoever runs that celebrity gossip site."

"Yule Berevit?" I asked.

"That's the one, Yule Believe It. I just don't know who's behind it," Cassidy continued.

"It's literally a man named Yule Berevit," I explained.

Cassidy looked at me quizzically.

"If you ask me, he deliberately mispronounces that surname to create the pun," Wiggles interjected.

"Is that a crime, officer?" Billie asked, her voice full of mockery.

Wiggles gave her a lopsided smile. "Not that I know of, ma'am. Getting back to the point, does anyone want to confess to speaking to the press?"

"You know your mother controlled how her life was reported. She'll be furious if any of you have contacted the press," Gabriel said. It seemed he was returning to his senses.

There was a flash of light out front as a patrol car and an ambulance arrived to take care of Peter Rhimes. Not that there was much they could do for him at this point, other than get his body out of the cold. We all looked out at the lights and were reminded that one person had died already.

Angel could be next.

Wiggles gave a grim smile and stood up. "Cornelius and I will go out and bring the team up to speed. Holly, can you handle this?"

I nodded, understanding what he was asking me. I was also pleased to take care of the inside jobs, where it was warm and free from dead bodies.

"I'll need to ask you some questions each. Dolly, I'll start with you. The rest of you stay right here."

I led Dolly into the great room's annex, which helpfully had glass sliding doors. I could interrogate people one by one without losing sight of the others.

Dolly was shaking with nerves as she sat down, and I reached out and gave her hand a quick squeeze.

"You can relax. I've asked you in here first because I think you're the one most likely to answer my questions honestly," I explained.

Dolly nodded, but her hands continued shaking. "I'll tell you everything you want to know."

"I'd like to get a bit of an understanding about your sisters. You seem like the quietest. Cassidy and Billie, did they give your mum trouble?"

Dolly shook her head. "Mama would never say that. She loves us all like a mama bear."

I gave a slow nod. "But Billie has cut her off and married a virtual stranger. She seems to have some real resentment towards Angel."

"She does. But she's the child. No matter how old we get, we'll always be mama's babies. That's what she tells us all the time, and it's true. I try to be as strong as she is, but it's not easy."

"What do you mean?"

"I mean Billie drives me nuts," Dolly admitted.

"She does?"

Dolly nodded and wiped a tear from her eye. "She's so selfish. No matter how much mama does, it's never enough for her."

"She does seem to have some kind of grudge against Angel," I agreed.

"It's always been the same. When she was little, she'd look in magazines for stories about mama and it drove her mad if she found articles that didn't mention her."

"But your mum tried to protect you all from the press, didn't she?"

"Exactly! Billie never wanted protecting. She's wanted to be a star since she was tiny."

"And Angel wouldn't allow it?"

Dolly shook her head furiously. "Mama says her own parents should never have let her become so famous as a child. She's always said if we want to enter the showbiz world when we're adults, that's up to us."

"And Billie does?"

"Yes, but she's got no talent," Dolly said, then gasped and covered her mouth. "Gosh, that sounds awful. Billie drives me mad, but I do love her, and of course she has talent. She just... she can't sing or dance or act. She wants to be famous but I have no clue what she could become famous for doing."

"Is that why marrying Cheep is part of her plan?"

Dolly glanced around and then leaned in close to me. "Can I tell you a secret?"

I nodded.

"This is Billie's third marriage," she confessed.

I tried to hide my surprise. Billie didn't look old enough to have been a bridesmaid three times, never mind a bride.

"I haven't heard about that in the press," I said.

"Mama made sure it was kept quiet. The weddings were annulled and the guys had to sign NDAs. After the second time, mama told her that if she pulled that stunt again, she'd be on her own."

"And Billie's smart enough to know there would be a lot of interest in her wedding," I said.

Dolly nodded. "She's been dreaming of selling her wedding photos to a magazine since she was tiny. She wants the attention. She lives for drama."

I took in what Dolly was telling me, and an idea formed. "Could Billie be behind this whole thing?"

"Kidnapping mama? But why would she do such a thing?"

"I don't know," I admitted. "It's just an idea. It seems like a coincidence that Billie shows up expectedly and then Angel is kidnapped. Maybe Billie's wedding didn't attract the attention she thought it would."

"She could be the poor upset daughter and speak to the press, that's what you're thinking?"

I shrugged. "It's just an idea. Let's talk about Cassidy. Tell me about her."

Dolly frowned. "What is there to say? She's my best friend. We're less than a year apart, you know. We could only be sisters through adoption, we're that close in age. She's like my twin."

"That must be hard for Billie."

Dolly nodded. "People often forget, Billie came last. Cass and I were adopted as babies, but Billie came when she was five. We were already a family without her. I don't think she's ever forgiven us for that."

"That's interesting. How about Gabriel, what's he like?"

Dolly giggled. "Apart from being hopelessly in love with mama?"

"He is?"

Dolly gave a full laugh then. "Oh, gosh, no! That's a joke! He's the only man who seems totally unaffected by all of her glamour and seduction. Not to mention he has a wife back home. And six children! Six!"

I snapped to attention. Somehow, I'd imagined Gabriel to have his whole life devoted to Angel and her needs.

"Yeah, it's wild, isn't it? He's been working for mama for twenty years, and if you ask me, he's a big part of why most of us have our feet on the ground."

"He's been a big part of your life?"

"We joke that he parented us more than his own kids," Dolly said with a smile. "You have to remember, we've never had a father figure. Mama has had relationships, but she's never allowed a man to join our family. Gabriel was the one who did that for us."

"And his wife doesn't mind sharing him?" I asked. It seemed wonderful, but odd, that a man with six children of his own could find time to be so involved with another family unit.

Dolly shrugged. "We've never met her. He likes to keep work and home separate."

"And had you met Mr Rhimes?" I asked.

Dolly shook her head. "Mama met with him regularly, but always at his offices. He never came to the house. Mama didn't involve us in all of those parts of her life."

"It sounds like she did a good job of letting you be regular kids," I said.

Dolly nodded. "That's exactly it. We went to school, came home and did our homework, played in the garden, laid the table for dinner. Mama's given us the best lives we could ever want."

"And what about these kidnap attempts? Do you know much about them?"

Dolly shook her head. "Only what I've read online. Mama never gave them any attention. Just a hazard of the job, that's what she said. Like if you're a robber you'll go to jail sometimes. It just comes with the job."

I raised my eyebrows. It was a bizarre comparison. Why would Angel use a criminal as a comparison?

"I think that was a little dig at her dad," Dolly explained.

"Oh, sure, Gilbert told me a little about that. He was taking her money?"

Dolly nodded, her eyes wide. "Can you imagine using your child as your own get rich quick scheme? What her parents did to her was awful."

I nodded my agreement. "Do you know if your mum has any enemies?"

Dolly gave a bitter laugh. "Nobody outside the family."

8

———

I asked Gabriel to speak to me next. I wanted to check on his state of shock. He took a seat and I listened to his heart beat, then took his blood pressure. I was glad I'd thought ahead and brought my doctor's bag out into the evening with me.

He was doing okay, but before I could ask him a question, my phone beeped with a message from August.

Are you okay????? The news is saying Angel's been kidnapped??? There's a ransom demand??? Let me know you're safe!!! Xoxo

"There's been a ransom?" I muttered under my breath. Gabriel was luckily still enough out of it that he didn't hear me.

My conversation with Dolly still fresh in my mind, I typed out a reply to my sister, asking her to see what intel she could dig up about Angel's parents.

Intel?????? Are we on a cop show now, sis?! Stop playing police and come home!!!!!!

I sighed at her reply, but before I could respond, three

dots appeared to show that she was typing again. Finally, she had seen sense and would help me.

You're already a doctor!! Let someone else cover the other emergency services!!!!!!

No, it turned out I was wrong. She just wasn't done criticising me. I was in too deep to give up, though. Angel was my patient, and that meant I had a duty of care towards her.

"Mr Howes, you want to tell me what you saw out there?" I asked as I drummed my fingers on the desk.

He blinked at me. "What I saw? I saw nothing!"

I blinked back at him. "A man is dead and your employer has been kidnapped, Gabriel. Whatever you're hiding, I suggest you quit it and start talking."

"Someone's finally managed to take her? Ha!" The man exclaimed, then burst into tears. I gave him a tissue, which he balled up in his hand as his tears ran freely down his face towards his flannel shirt.

"You know about the other attempts?"

"Of course I do! Who do you think checks her emails and opens her post?"

"I'm guessing, you?"

"Ding ding ding! The lady wins!"

I took a deep breath. The thing with diagnosing whether someone's acting crazy because of shock, is you need to know their normal personality to make a comparison. Sure, Gabriel seemed pretty out of it, but maybe he was always that way.

"You're reaction's a little..."

"Surprising? Ha!" Gabriel exclaimed as he began to rock in the chair a little. His flannel strained over his stomach.

"Well, yes. She could be in danger, you realise?"

Gabriel crossed his legs and raised his eyebrows. "She's always in danger. Every damn day there's a mad man ready to grab her and hurt her. You think everyone who wants to hurt her publicises their kidnap plans? Nuh uh. The real crazies are the ones who don't give a warning."

"And who do you think could be behind this? I get the impression you know her well."

"Better than anyone else in the world," he said, with no air of pride or exaggeration. In fact, did he look a little bemused? A tad exhausted?

"She had enemies?"

"Oh, no!" Gabriel exclaimed. "The opposite. She has a lot of people who think they love her so much they want her to belong to them. It's the crazy fans we're scared of, not the people who hate her music."

"So she does have enemies," I pushed.

Gabriel appeared genuinely puzzled, as if the idea had never occurred to him before. "Do you think someone wants to hurt her?"

"I think that's a risk," I admitted. I was surprised I was having to spell it out for him. Whoever was behind this plot had already killed old Peter Rhimes. The thought made me shudder. There was something indecent about killing a man wearing a suit and brogues.

"Well, I mean..."

"Listen to me. Angel's in danger, and you're the person who knows her best! You need to start talking!"

He looked up at my harsh tone and promptly began to cry again.

"Gabriel, I'm sorry. It's just..." I leaned in and softened my voice. "Whatever you can tell me may help save her."

He took a shuddering breath and glanced around to see who was watching. Fortunately, everyone out in the room seemed lost in their own thoughts and nobody was watching us.

"If I had to point a finger at anyone, it would be Angel's dad."

I sat back, stunned. "You think he'd do such a thing?"

Gabriel scoffed and ran his fingers through his hair. "That man is a monster. He bled her dry when she was younger. He pushed her too hard, said yes to every offer she had. She was like a zombie."

"He was her manager?"

"He controlled everything, and he was stealing from her. She should be a very, very rich woman right now."

I tried not to look surprised. Everything about Angel suggested to me that she was indeed a very, very rich woman. Maybe she and I had different ideas about what that meant.

"You know he went to prison?" Gabriel asked. I did know that, Gilbert had told me about it, but I looked surprised so Gabriel would tell me his version.

He took a deep breath. "He was submitting expenses, getting backhanders from people, all sorts. He'd book a private gig for $60k but only thirty would ever make it on to the balance sheet."

"He really did that to his daughter?"

"Unbelievable, right? The accountants figured it out eventually. The numbers didn't add up one time too many, and his excuses stopped fooling anyone. He served a stretch all right, but nowhere near long enough."

"That's awful," I murmured.

"You know the worst thing? If he'd just asked, she would have given him as much as he wanted. Angel's generous to a fault. She'd see herself poor rather than say no to someone. But he had to go behind her back. Can you imagine that? Finding out your own dad's been stealing from you?"

We sat in stunned silence for a few seconds as I processed what Gabriel had told me. Poor Angel.

"Wait. You say you suspect him of doing this. Isn't he in prison?"

Gabriel snickered. "That's the thing. He was let out last week. Why do you think Angel's moved?"

9

———

As Gabriel and I returned to the great room, Wiggles and Cornelius were just returning from outside. I made my way across the room to speak to the chief of police.

By the way he was waddling, it looked as though Cornelius was in desperate need of a toilet. He disappeared down the hallway towards the bathroom.

"Mr Rhimes has been taken away," Wiggles informed me.

"So, he is dead?" I asked, although I already knew the answer to that question.

Wiggles nodded, then indicated towards the room, where everyone sat in stony silence. "You get anything out of them?"

"I'm still making my way through speaking to them all, but Gabriel told me something that is worrying."

"You don't say?"

I nodded. "Angel's dad is fresh out of prison, and he suggested that she had moved away in an attempt to hide from him."

Wiggles stared at me. "Her own dad?"

"He was stealing from her apparently. That's why he went to prison."

"Revenge is always a strong motive. You think Mr Rhimes just got in the way?"

I shrugged. "I'll keep speaking to people, but the father could be worth a look into."

Wiggles nodded. "Leave it with me. If he's fresh out of prison he'll be on licence. I'll see whether he's missed any appointments."

I gave him a smile. "Thank you. Did you find any clues out there?"

Wiggles grimaced. "You know the problem with the snow..."

"It hides evidence. I was worried about that."

"We can say he was hit with a blunt object, though. And there were candy cane fragments spread around him, marking the shape of his body."

"Candy canes? You mean the killer... decorated?" I gasped.

Wiggles nodded. "I hadn't thought of it that way, but I guess so."

"Have you seen anything like that before?" I asked.

He shook his head. "Some killers leave a calling card, something that signifies the killing as being theirs. It's not something I've come across, but I've read plenty about it."

"What would that kind of behaviour say about the murderer?"

Wiggles blew out a long breath. "It's been a long time since my training..."

"You must remember something!"

Wiggles nodded. "It suggests the crime was premeditated."

"You mean it wasn't a random killing and then the murderer realised they had some candy canes in their pocket?"

"Exactly. It's more likely that it was all planned, that our killer was cool and calm, and that they took some pleasure in what they did."

I frowned.

"That's not what you want to hear?"

"It just doesn't fit. I was working on the assumption that Angel was the real target."

Wiggles raised his eyebrows. "It could be a smokescreen."

"Or maybe it's Peter who had an enemy."

I turned and looked at the people in the room. All of them were suspects for Angel's kidnapping, but they were all in the room when Peter was outside being killed.

"I'm going to speak to another suspect."

10

Billie followed me into the annex room reluctantly, and only after a drawn out farewell kiss with her new husband. As she took a sip of water, I noticed that her lipstick was smudged.

"It's cute that you play police. I used to play games like that as a kid too," she said with a sneer.

I gave her a tight smile. "I help the police from time to time."

"But I don't have to speak to you, right? You can't issue a warrant and arrest me?"

"I can't. But I can ask Wiggles to come in and do that if that's what you'd prefer."

"Maybe I would."

I nodded. "You know that an arrest shows on your record? I'm sure you wouldn't want the press finding out that you were interrogated about your mum's disappearance?"

She shifted in her seat. The saying went that there was no such thing as bad publicity, but I didn't believe that, and I didn't think Billie would either. She was a young woman desperate to start writing her own narrative, and kidnapper didn't seem like the vibe she was aiming at.

"You work out?" I asked.

The question clearly confused her, and she had nodded before she realised. "No comment."

I shrugged. "I'm asking because you look toned. I keep saying I'll work out more, but it's hard to start the habit. That's the hardest part, I think. Starting the habit? Not to mention resisting the mince pies and hot chocolates. Phew, this place is amazing but not great for my waistline."

Billie gave me a look of disdain that I suspect she had perfected as a teenager and then never grew out of. "I've always exercised. It used to be the one thing mom and I did together."

"That's really lovely."

Billie shook her head. "She was always practising. She makes up most of her dance routines herself, you know? And of course she can never wear a full length top for any of her shows, so she's basically been maintaining a six pack since she was thirteen."

"That's incredible," I admitted. I had imagined Angel to be one of the lucky ones; gifted with a perfect voice. I'd never considered the hard work she had to put in for each of her shows. Or to keep her body perfect.

"Yeah, well, when I arrived in the family, Cassidy and Dolly were already so tight. I figured I'd make mom my best friend instead. We went to the dance studio together. I know all the dances."

"Is that what you wanted to do? Grow up and be a dancer?" I asked.

She shook her head. "I didn't know what I wanted to be. Just a wife and a mother, I think."

"And now that dream's coming true. Congratulations, by the way. On your wedding."

She batted my compliments away with her hand. "Oh, don't. I know nobody's happy about that. They all think I'm just a train wreck. But Cheep is really sweet. Everyone seems to think the tattoos and the rap music mean he's a gangster, but you know who that guy's hero is? His gran! Literally!"

I smiled. "He seems really nice."

Billie gazed at me, perhaps hearing the sincerity in my voice. "Thanks. He is. But you've not asked me in here for marriage advice. You think I can help you find mom?"

"I don't know, but it's possible."

"Okay then. Ask me whatever you need to."

"Thank you. Let's start with your mom's enemies. Does she have any?"

Billie cocked her head. "Aren't we starting with Peter Rhimes? He's the victim here."

Interesting.

"He is, but it's possible he was only killed because he was in the wrong place at the wrong time. Whoever did this, it's your mom they really wanted."

"And now they've got her," Billie whispered.

"It looks like it. Who would do this to her, Billie?"

Billie shook her head. "I don't know! Everyone loves my mom! That's why my life is hard, because I'll always just be in her shadow! Nobody would ever want to hurt her!"

"But that's not true. She's been plagued by kidnap threats."

Billie scoffed. "Sure, people want to kidnap her. But not hurt her. Have you seen the kind of kidnap threats she gets?"

I shook my head.

"It's all like, let me whisk you away from the press and show you my collection of Angel posters, or let me take you home to my parents so you can taste my mother's casserole. These people don't want to hurt her. They want to stop her hurting!" Billie gasped then, as if she had said more than she ever meant to.

"And why is she hurting?"

Billie began to cry. "Isn't that obvious? She was the cash cow for her whole family growing up. You know she doesn't speak to any of them? Not her dad, of course, but her mom and her sister were in on it too. They just hid their tracks better. No prison time for them! But mom's never really got over the way they betrayed her."

"That seems understandable," I said. "Does she ever hear from them?"

Billie rolled her eyes. "Mom would never tell any of us kids if she did. We just don't speak about them."

"I've heard that her dad has just been released from prison. Do you know anything about that?"

Billie shook her head. "She wouldn't tell us."

"Are you sure? Wouldn't she want you to know so you could all be careful?"

Billie looked out into the great room. Cheep was gazing at her and when he saw her looking, blew her a kiss.

"Isn't he great?" Billie asked.

"He seems like a really nice guy." I agreed. "It must be hard meeting people. Do you ever worry whether people are just trying to get close to your mom?"

Billie jerked back as if I'd slapped her. I'd clearly touched a nerve. "I am a person, you know? I have a personality and interests all of my own. I'm a pretty great person, actually. This little pretend interview is rubbish. I'm out!"

And with that, my prime suspect jumped up from her seat, and left the room.

As she did so, Cornelius passed by, saw that I was alone, and wandered in. He was glued to his phone, as usual.

"We have a problem," he murmured.

"Another one?"

He held the phone out to me. "The story's broke."

"I already know that," I said.

He shook his head and his jowls wobbled. "Not the kidnap."

I recognised the gaudy colours of Yule Berevit's website, Yule Believe It. According to Gilbert, the man was a big fan of Angel's, although the cynic in me suspected he was a fan of anyone who would attract big visitor numbers to his site.

ANGEL'S VILLAIN STRIKES: CELEB'S LAWYER KILLED!!! was the headline. I groaned.

"Who told him?" I asked.

Cornelius shrugged his broad shoulders. "A source close to the star, that's all he ever says. It's important in ground-breaking journalism that sources know their identities will be protected."

"This is hardly groundbreaking journalism," I muttered.

"A lot of people care about Angel, lassie. They'll be invested in this story!"

"They'll be ringing up with nonsense tips and trampling all over evidence," I said, and I got up from my chair, walked back into the great room, and looked out the window. Sure enough, at the edge of the property's perimeter, behind the candy cane fence, was a crowd of people and elves.

Gilbert followed my gaze. "Angel's Angels are here."

I shook my head, went to the front door, and scanned the crowd. Could one of them be the murderer? It was a common trick, becoming a helper, joining a search party, befriending the family. As my eyes adjusted, I saw that one of the crowd was waving at me enthusiastically, and groaned.

"Holly! Dear! Shall I come inside?" Yule Berevit shouted across at me.

I shook my head and allowed the door to slam louder than was necessary.

"You seem frustrated," Wiggles said. He was tucking in to a fresh plate of the charcuterie board food. Police investigation was hungry work.

"I feel out of depth. This isn't my world. I don't know anything about Angel's celebrity life."

"Maybe speak to someone who does," Wiggles offered.

I resisted the urge to suggest he put down the plate of food and do a little of the investigation himself. He had stood out in the cold with Peter Rhimes' body for a good while. He deserved a plate of food.

"Actually," I said, "that's it. You're a genius!"

He grinned at me as he stuffed a slice of salami in his mouth.

"Gilbert," I called. The elf was sitting on a settee with perfect posture, his gaze focused on Wiggles, who was serving himself food. It was clearly killing the elf not to go over and help. "I have a job for you!"

Gilbert beamed at me and scurried across, but instead of going into the annex room, I wandered out of the great room and he followed. We walked in silence and I popped my head in each room we passed until finally, we came to Angel's bedroom.

It was neat and tidy, with the bed made and all of her cosmetics arranged on an ornate dressing table. A negligee was folded tidily on her bed, and on the bedside table was a capsule of tablets, a Joan Didion book, and a pair of reading glasses. An almost empty glass of water, imprinted with Angel's pink lipstick, stood on top of the book.

"Is this her room?" Gilbert squealed. I turned and gave him a warning glance and he pretended to zip up his mouth.

"I need your help," I whispered.

"Me? You want me to help you investigate? Oh-em-gee! Yes, sirree!"

"I just... I don't know the first thing about Angel's life. Can you give me like a potted history?"

Gilbert gave me the intense gaze he usually saved for waiting for feedback as we tasted a new recipe of his. "When you say potted history, do you mean like from birth, or becoming a celebrity, or..."

"Just tell me everything," I begged.

"Yes, ma'am. Okay, Angel Albright was born to a regular couple, she was discovered when she was six years old but her parents refused to let her act then. She was wanted as a child model, again the parents said no. Then she hits the scene when she's fifteen with a raunchy song and a little sexpot's outfit in the cult hit movie, *Cheerleader*."

I knew the song, and the video. It was impossible not to. "So what happened. Her parents were against it, and then they weren't?"

Gilbert grinned. He was in his element. "Her dad's business failed. That's commonly accepted as the main reason. The interesting thing is, she has a younger sister, and she was acting when she was ten. So there's the business failing, the young sister gets an acting gig, and then Angel's sent out to work."

"I don't know the sister?" I admitted.

Gilbert rolled his eyes. "She's a snake. She never amounted to much herself, but she's got three memoirs, all about Angel. The thing is, Angel is the whole family's cash cow. Like that first video, Angel has said how uncomfortable she was with it. It was way too mature for a fifteen year old kid, but the dad was in charge then, and he wanted to go for shock value. He was always that way, whatever would get the biggest impact, the most interest, and earn the most money."

"Where's the mum in all of this?" I asked.

"Not as involved. She was a teacher. She kept that job until her husband had stolen enough money from Angel that they were set for life. They had the mansion, the fancy cars, even a yacht at one point. So she gave up the job. Angel had adopted Cassidy and Dolly by this point, so the mum was helping with childcare, kinda travelling around with Angel, making that her life."

"And then what happened? What went wrong?"

"Angel started to get sick. She was burnt out, we could all see it. There were chats on the message forum about it. We were all worried about her. But if anything her schedule got more intense. She was doing two shows a day, every day. She started to make mistakes, she collapsed on stage once. It was all falling apart."

"I remember her collapsing," I said. I hadn't remembered it until Gilbert said it, but as soon as he did, I could see the clips from the news. Midway through a song, pouring with sweat, Angel had wobbled a bit on those impossible high heels, and then collapsed. The crowds had cheered, thinking it was part of the show, and it took the medics more than five minutes to go to her. *If she'd been dying she'd have been dead,* that's what I'd thought at the time.

Gilbert nodded. "That was really the start of the end for her dad. He had her back on stage that very night, and twice the next day, and on and on. She was clearly too sick to perform but he didn't care. The accountant was starting to suspect and that was the thing that convinced him to take a real close look at things. It turned out, the dad had overcommitted himself financially."

"How is that possible if he was stealing so much?" I asked.

Gilbert laughed. "I know, right? It's hard for us to imagine, but his lifestyle then was costing a million dollars a month. More if he wanted to go on holiday or get a new car or invest in another stupid business, and he always wanted to do those things. It all came out in court. He was spending the million a month on essentials - ha! - and his total average spend was three million a month."

"Wowzers," I said. I'd always imagined if I'd ever be lucky enough to win a million on the lottery, it would be enough to set up me and August for life. And there was Angel's dad, probably spending that much as if it was small change.

"So the dad sounds like a con man," I said.

"Oh, 100%."

"But could he be dangerous?"

Gilbert considered my question and then reluctantly shook his head. "It would be nice and tidy if he was, but I don't see it. He had no criminal record before the fraud. He did an interview from prison, actually, last year. Claimed to have found God."

"Let me guess. He's sorry and just wants a fresh start."

Gilbert scrunched up his nose as if a bad smell had entered the room. "That man deserves no such thing."

11

I asked Gilbert to return to the great room, and I stayed in Angel's bedroom alone.

It was surreal to believe that I was in the bedroom of one of the biggest modern day celebrities. I sat on her bed and touched her Egyptian cotton sheets. I inspected the Joan Didion book and saw that it was a first edition, personally signed and inscribed to Angel. The almost-empty water glass was Cartier.

Was there anything normal about Angel's life?

Suddenly, I remembered Peter Rhimes' eagerness to find me and have Angel set up as a client. As her lawyer, he would be expected to sort things for her, and some of them would be urgent. But finding a doctor would only be urgent if she had an ongoing medical issue. Or was undergoing some kind of testing or diagnosis.

My eyes flicked across to the pill bottle on the bedside table. It wasn't a breach of confidentiality for me to check what they were. The information would be readily available to me on her patient file.

I picked up the pill and read the label, and gasped.

Finally, there was something normal about the megastar. The pills were the most commonly prescribed. Pills I had prescribed day after day after day. I could list off the possible side effects from memory.

It turned out, despite everything, like eight million other people in the UK, Angel Albright was depressed.

I felt the weight in the room intensify. It seemed that no matter how successful, rich or popular a person was, happiness was guaranteed for nobody. Considering Angel's family history, it was no surprise that she had sought a little medical assistance.

I returned the pills to the bedside table and pulled open the drawers. The top drawer was full to bursting with notebooks, and I took them out and flicked through them one by one. Lyrics filled every page, some of them a random line, or a list of rhyming words, and other pages containing complete songs.

The smallest notebook of all was right at the bottom, hidden from view by several larger ones. I took a breath and opened it, and found that I was looking at Angel's diary.

I skimmed through the pages, not wanting to read anything that I didn't have a reason to see. Most entries were fairly dull, a record of her sleep, any dreams she had had, her weight, what she ate, and a rather cryptic plus or minus sign.

Was she monitoring whether each day was good or bad, or something else entirely?

I flicked to the back of the notebook but the last entry was from a week earlier.

I shuddered as I read her words.

Today daddy gets to go home. Or will he come to see me???

12

___

Downstairs, the atmosphere was bleak.

I felt unsure about whether I could do anything more to help with the investigation. The most likely culprit appeared to be Angel's dad, and we had no evidence that he was even in town.

I approached Wiggles.

"I think I've reached a dead end," I apologised.

"Nonsense. You're doing great. Better than me at any rate. Keeping that crowd away from the house is getting harder," Wiggles admitted.

I followed his gaze out through the windows and saw that the crowds out by the fence had grown in size and volume.

"They're chanting?"

He nodded.

I moved to the front door and cracked it open an inch. As soon as I did, their jumbled noise became clear.

WHAT DO WE WANT? JUSTICE FOR ANGEL
WHEN DO WE WANT IT? NOW

"Is that the best they can do? I used to sing that song as a child about wanting chips for dinner," I muttered.

"You know, some kind of official statement might be needed," Wiggles' cheeks flushed as he spoke.

"You don't sound keen?"

He shrugged. "I just never like public attention."

I watched him, wide eyed. It wasn't that long ago I had seen him take to the ice in a glittering skintight leotard. He'd certainly got some public attention then.

"I could talk to them," I offered.

"It really should be me," he said, to my relief. I didn't like public attention either, whether it be speaking to crowds of concerned fans, or bearing all in a skintight, sequinned number.

"You'll do fine," I said.

Wiggles nodded, and I followed him down the long, weaving drive of Holiday Haven until we reached the crowds. Yule Berevit had a front row position, of course, and by the time we reached him, he had pulled a microphone from his shoulder bag and seemed to be recording us, using a phone on a long device.

"Is that a selfie stick?" I scoffed.

"The first rule of journalism. Always be prepared for a story," he flashed a bright white smile that I imagined was costing him more than a tube of toothpaste to maintain.

Wiggles cleared his throat. "Ladies and gents, elfs and folk, I understand your concern."

"Is Angel dead?" Someone called out from the crowd.

"Is it right that she's been kidnapped by Big Foot?" Another voice came.

Goodness. I thought I saw the extremes of humanity, with the Google-diagnosing I saw in my clinic. What gossip columns were these people reading?!

"We have an ongoing police investigation, and this house and its grounds are crime scenes. I'm here to ask for your co-operation in maintaining the integrity of this land," Wiggles explained.

I watched as a large, burly man pushed his way through the crowd until he was right next to Yule Berevit, who had directed the phone away from Wiggles, and to this man.

"Where is she?" The man barked. His face was bright red and a large scar spanned the length of his right cheek.

"All I can say for now is that Angel Albright appears to have been kidnapped. There has been one fatality this evening, a gentleman named Peter Rhimes who we understand was Ms Albright's lawyer. We are treating that death as suspicious. We welcome tips and information on our hot line, 0800 CANDY CANE. That's all for now, folks."

"Where is she?" The large man repeated, and I watched with interest as he directed his pleas straight to Yule Berevit's phone screen.

"Oh, no," I muttered.

The man waited until he had the attention of the whole crowd, then pointed his finger towards Wiggles.

"You!" He cried. "You tell me right now, where is my daughter?"

A short woman with a bouffant and shoulder pads pushed her way through the crowds and grabbed his arm. She seemed out of breath, which was unsurprising as she seemed to have travelled all the way from the 1980s.

"Mr and Mrs Albright?" Wiggles asked.

The couple nodded. The woman straightened her hair a little.

"Is she safe? That's all we care about!" The woman exclaimed. She spoke straight into Yule Berevit's phone, then grabbed her husband's face. "We should make an appeal for information."

A large boo rippled through the crowds.

"The appeal should be by her loved ones, not you con artists!" Someone shouted. The crowd roared their agreement.

"Now, now. Let's not be hasty," Yule Berevit urged. I could almost see the cogs whirring in his head as he created a headline for their video. "Let's give it a try."

"You'll do no such thing. Any appeal for information will be organised by the police, only if and when we consider it appropriate. Now, you two? Follow me."

Angel's parents had the decency to look at the ground as they followed Wiggles towards Holiday Haven. I decided to bring up the rear, mainly to ensure that Yule Berevit wasn't trying to sneak in with us.

"Oh, isn't this place darling? It reminds me of the skiing trip we took back in 2015," Mrs Albright said as she assessed the grandness of Holiday Haven.

"That trip was a bust. No ice for the Champagne! And they dared to call it a five star resort," Mr Albright complained.

As we drew close to Holiday Haven, Wiggles swung a left. There was a wooden cabin at the side of the building, no doubt used to house outdoor furniture, or a hot tub, or whatever else five star accommodation offered. Having never stayed in one, I was ill-equipped to guess.

As Wiggles pushed open the creaky wooden door, a wave of warmth enveloped him and the rest of us, like a snug embrace from an old friend. The dimly lit interior of the wooden cabin revealed its enchanting secret: a hidden sauna, a delightful surprise for any weary travellers who could afford the stay.

The walls were adorned with rustic, hand-carved wooden panels, depicting whimsical forest scenes that seemed to come alive in the soft glow of the lanterns. A collection of antique copper pots and kettles hung from the ceiling, their surfaces gleaming in the flickering light.

The sauna itself was a masterpiece of craftsmanship, its wooden benches worn smooth with time and countless saunas past. The air was heavy with the soothing scent of cedar, a fragrance that invited relaxation. Cozy, plaid towels were neatly stacked in a wicker basket, and a row of fluffy bathrobes hung on hooks, each embroidered with a charming woodland animal.

And there, collapsed on the far bench, was the unmistakable, and lifeless figure of Angel Albright.

13

It was no micro nap. I realised that quickly.

A quick examination of her pulse showed that she had clearly lost consciousness, and who could say how long she had been out cold for in the raging heat of the sauna.

Between us, we carried her out into the frigid temperature of the grounds.

"Is that her?" A voice came. I had no time to consider who had followed us down the private path, although I hoped it wasn't Yule Berevit, who would no doubt have snapped photos and uploaded them to his site in an instant. Let Wiggles deal with whoever was trespassing.

Before we reached Holiday Haven, Angel began to stir. Her eyes were glassy, her hair matted and stuck to the side of her face.

"Am I dead?" She croaked.

I shook my hand, reached across and squeezed her hand to reassure her. "Let's get you inside and we'll have a chat."

"Angel!" Someone shouted. A gruff, desperate voice. I

felt a wave of anger ripple through my stomach but didn't know why.

"Daddy?" She called.

We reached the door and I finally turned. Mr and Mrs Albright stood before us, as if they were some relic from the nativity and needed an inn for the night. Only one person could grant them safe passage, and I felt pleased the decision wasn't mine. I couldn't trust myself to be as generous as they were asking.

Angel, it seemed, was a kinder woman than me. "You can't stay out in the cold."

And so the decision was made simply. Outside was cold. Angel could offer them warmth. I wondered if she had a fever and was making a rational decision or not.

"Before anything else happens, I need to examine your daughter," I addressed the wayward parents, my face stern.

They nodded and clutched each other. They were certainly giving the appearance of two contrite adults, but I wasn't ready to believe the act just yet. Not least because Mrs Albright was adorned in a large set of pearls and Mr Albright's watch was clearly from a designer brand.

I led Angel into the mud room, according to the sign on the door. In reality, the mud room was a whole suite including a wet room, a laundry room with a rail of clothes hangers and some hi-tech iron that looked more complicated than my car, and then a sitting room where I presumed people changed into their outdoor clothes.

The rich sure could fill a big space with any number of rooms us everyday folk managed fine without. Although I could see the appeal of a dedicated utility room.

Angel took a seat and offered me a smile.

"How do you feel?" I asked as I took her pulse again. It

was fine, back to normal, and her eyes were alert. She didn't have a fever.

"It's the strangest thing. I don't know what happened," she implored me, her eyes wide.

"Well, we don't know either. It seemed as though you'd been kidnapped. You remember there was a threat?"

She nodded. "But there always is, right?"

I sighed. "You have to start taking these things seriously. A man is dead, Angel."

She gasped and I realised my mistake. Her memory may not be complete, and I had just revealed the fatality in an incredibly insensitive way.

"I'm sorry. It's your lawyer. He... he's dead, Angel," I said.

She shook her head. "Poor Peter."

"What do you remember?"

"I remember Gabriel coming in covered in blood. That's why I ran."

"You mean you weren't kidnapped?"

She laughed. "Of course not. Who could get to me here? I just didn't want any other innocent people getting hurt because of me. I figured if someone wanted to harm me, I'd make sure I was alone so they could just come straight for me."

I considered her words and found that I had to give it to her. Her family said she had always controlled the media attention, and yet again she had managed it. She created the kidnapping news herself. What better way to put off any wannabe kidnapper than the idea that someone else had already beat them to it?

"You're a genius," I murmured. "But the sauna?"

She shrugged. "I thought a place like this would be full of outbuildings. Usually they are. There'll be a stables and a gym and an indoor pool. That old sauna was the only thing I could find here!"

I tried to ignore the idea that Holiday Haven's luxury facilities had been found lacking, and kept my focus on what she was telling me.

"But your phone…"

"Yeah. I tossed it in the snow. Let me guess, Find my Friends was the first thing you guys tried?"

"It was," I admitted.

"Oh, don't look so serious. I was trying to protect everyone, not fool them. Peter could be such a bore, but I'd never want him dead. Even if he had been driving me crazy this last week."

"Driving you crazy how?" I asked.

"He had some convoluted tax investment thing he wanted me to agree to. I didn't understand it. I just couldn't get my head around what exactly the investment was. All he could show me was payments going into a shell account. He was quoting tax loopholes to me, but I guess I'm not smart enough."

"Is that unusual? That he'd be pushing you to do something like that?"

"Oh, no! He's always pushing me to do things with my money that I'd rather not do. It was all, file these papers, meet this deadline, pay this tax. Ugh. What a bore."

"But did he give you investment advice?"

She stopped and gazed at me and I could almost see the lightbulb go off above her head. "As a matter of fact, no. He's a lawyer not a financial advisor. Or, he was."

"Isn't it a coincidence that he was pushing you to do something new with your money right as your dad was released from prison?"

Angel rolled her eyes. "I did think the same, but whatever you're thinking, it's not that. Peter couldn't stand my dad. He's a father too, you see. In fact, his daughter's sick. He loved her so much. He couldn't understand how a father could treat a daughter so badly."

"His daughter's sick?"

She nodded. "They were trying to get her across to America for some operation or something... he got upset when I asked about it."

I cocked my head to the side. "If she needed an operation, why hadn't he taken her across for it?"

Angel shrugged. "I guess she must have been too sick to travel."

"That's awful," I murmured. "Now, we need to talk about your parents."

Her cheeks flushed. "I tried to visit daddy once, you know."

"You did? Why?"

"Oh, I don't know. I think I wanted to see him and just ask why he did it."

"And what did he say?"

"I never made it. There was this very handsome prison guard. You wouldn't believe the things we did in the cells!"

I had to laugh. "Come on, let's get you out there. You're sure you're okay with your parents being here?"

"I like to keep my friends close and my enemies closer," she straightened her back and her impressive bosom stuck out in a defiant pose of pride, but the smile she gave was weak. Deep down, I suspected that Angel Albright was just a daughter desperate for her parents' love.

I gave her shoulder a squeeze. "Let's go and solve this murder."

14

Everyone was gathered around in the great room and several were filling plates with offerings from the charcuterie board, which appeared to be never ending in its supply of fancy cheeses and foreign meats.

I cleared my throat and a few people looked across at me, but most continued what they were doing. Lil Cheep sat with his tattooed hands clasped on his lap, his attention as bright as if I were a teacher about to begin assembly. He really did have the most excellent manners.

Gilbert saw the determination on my face and dashed across to my side.

"You know who did it," he whispered.

"I do."

"Please tell me it's not Angel. I couldn't handle it if she went to prison. That would be a real test of my morals. To love the singer or hate the criminal! How could a mere elf choose?"

I cocked a smile. I suspected he would have little difficulty in making the decision.

"I'd like everyone's attention, please," I said. Conversations in the room hushed.

"Your little amateur sleuth game comes to an end?" Billie sneered.

Wiggles shot her a stern look but she simply rolled her eyes.

"We have all of the necessary people here now. At first it seemed that Peter Rhimes was a random victim, killed for being in the wrong place at the wrong time. We assumed that the killer wanted Angel, because of the kidnap threat and her celebrity."

"Who'd want to kill that old man? It's more likely someone would be bored to death by him," Billie muttered.

"Exactly. He was such a formal, old-fashioned man. It was hard to consider that anything about him was controversial enough for him to lose his life over."

"You're right! Peter never did a thing wrong by anyone," Angel insisted.

"I'm sure you're right, ordinarily. But then you told me about his daughter. His sick daughter. You said she was too sick to travel to America for the operation needed to save her life, but that didn't make sense to me. If that's where the lifesaving operation is, a father would do anything to get a daughter there."

"Oh," Angel said, her face a question.

"There was something else going on, Angel. Something that your long-term fame has allowed you to forget, or never need to know about. I'm a doctor, remember. I have my share of patients asking me for medications that aren't yet in general use. I have patients who beg me to refer them to other areas where the waiting lists are shorter. And I have patients who sadly never get the referrals or the treatments they need. You know what all of those people have in common?"

Angel shook her head.

"They don't have the money to get what they need privately."

"Peter couldn't afford the operation?" Dolly murmured.

"That's nonsense. If he needed money, he'd have asked," Angel said with a laugh.

"No he wouldn't. He was too proud," Gabriel said.

"Proud? Rubbish! I'd have helped him, no questions asked."

"It's hard for a man to ask a younger woman to help," Angel's dad said with a grimace.

"Don't make this about you, daddy," Angel spat.

"Peter came to you, didn't he?" I asked.

Angel's dad looked at the floor. "We kept in touch. I wrote to him every quarter from jail. I think he only replied out of courtesy. He had those old fashioned manners. He never told me anything about you, Angel. That was a line he wouldn't cross. But he told me about his daughter."

"When was this?" I asked.

He shrugged. "A few weeks ago? I replied right away with my commiserations. I told him there was a scheme I'd heard about on the grapevine, something that could get him the money he needed quick. He replied to say he was interested."

"And then he presented Angel with the information you'd prepared for him. You knew Angel wasn't confident about managing her own money. You were the one who made her lose confidence in that!"

"You tricked me, daddy."

"I needed something to set me up for my release. I had

restitution to pay and I needed to support me and your mother. This scheme let me do that."

"And you've managed pretty well if the jewellery's anything to go by," I quipped.

"People find me very believable. It was sufficient to allow me to have enough ready when I was released."

"And then what happened? Did Peter have a twinge of guilt? Was he going to tell everyone about it?" Dolly asked.

"What happened to his daughter?" Angel asked.

"She got on a plane the day I was released. She will have had the operation by now," Angel's dad explained.

Angel let out a long breath. "Well, that's one good thing. Why wouldn't Peter have just asked me for the money? This is such a mess! Why did you have to kill him, daddy?"

"What? I didn't kill him! I might have dabbled in some creative accounting here and there but nothing I've ever done has actually hurt someone! That's not me!"

"Well someone killed poor Peter!"

"Yes, someone killed him. But it wasn't your dad," I said. "Peter was killed by someone loyal to you who discovered the way he had been defrauding you."

Angel looked across the room, taking in the people she was surrounded by. Her parents. Her daughters.

"I believe the person who killed Peter saw the act as a way of ingratiating himself into your family, Angel."

"You are not suggesting Cheep did this!" Billie ordered. All eyes turned to Cheep, whose cheeks had flamed pink. He studied something on the floor rather than meet anyone's gaze.

The young star then grabbed Billie's hand in his and kissed it. He murmured what sounded like an apology.

"You killed a man to impress my mother? Ugh! This is so

typical! Why do these things always happen to me?!" Billie exclaimed as she scooted away from him.

"It wasn't him," I said.

Cheep grinned at me, almost as if he had had doubts himself over his guilt or innocence.

"Then who was it? Everyone here is family," Angel said.

Dolly cast an eye towards her grandparents and fixed them with a scowl. It was clear that not everyone considered *them* to be family.

"Why don't you explain what happened?" I prompted as I levelled my gaze at the killer.

He let out a sigh.

"It was you?" Angel asked. "But why?"

Gabriel took a deep breath and met her gaze. He attempted to rise to his feet, to go to her, but his legs were too shaky to support him.

"But he's been a wreck since he found the body!" Cassidy exclaimed.

"Yes. Finding a body can cause that shock. But so can murdering a person," I said.

Gabriel buried his head in his hands and began to cry. His soft sobs were the only noise in the room, until Angel's dad cleared his throat. "Well done for working it all out! Let's get this man removed and we can get on with a nice, family Christmas, eh?"

Angel stomped across the room to him and folded her arms across her chest as she stared at him. "Daddy, I only invited you in in case you were the killer."

"You'd honestly think I could..."

"I'd put nothing past you. But since this crime is surprisingly not because of you, you can leave now. Go on! Both of you!"

Mr and Mrs Albright gave each other stunned glances

and Mrs Albright began to play meditatively with the pearls around her neck.

"We'll be going then," Mr Albright said, as if the decision had been theirs.

"I've got some colleagues waiting in a patrol car outside," Wiggles said. "They'll have some questions for you about this Ponzi scheme you're running."

"That's nonsense!"

Wiggles shrugged. "In that case, the questions won't take more than a minute."

With deep frowns etched on their faces, Mr and Mrs Albright left, and full attention returned to Gabriel.

His sobs slowed, then drew to a gasping halt. "I did it for you, Angel."

"Me? I've never asked you to hurt anyone! I love - well, I was quite fond of Peter. Even if he was dreadfully dull," Angel said.

"He was working in cahoots with your dad and I couldn't stand to see you betrayed. Not again."

"Why didn't you just tell me?" Angel asked.

"I was going to. That's why I was on my way here. I followed Peter here. We argued and I made it clear he was going to confess everything or I would. We got into a fight," Gabriel said, and as he spoke he pulled up the sleeve of his red flannel shirt. There was a deep wound on his arm that had bled, unnoticed, onto his bloody clothes.

He hadn't just been in shock, then. He was injured, too.

"That looks nasty," I said as I stepped closer to him.

"Why do you care? I'm a murderer!"

"You're still entitled to medical attention. Sit still," I commanded, and I examined the wound closer. As is common, it had bled excessively. The injury itself wasn't as bad as it first looked, but the cut was deep, and in it I was sure I saw... "He bit you?"

Gabriel nodded. "I panicked when he did that. I grabbed the first thing I could see, it was that huge candy cane. I just whacked him... I didn't mean to... he just fell to the ground and that was it, he was dead."

"Then you didn't murder him," Dolly said, her law studies kicking in. "It's manslaughter!"

"What does it matter what it's called? A man is dead because of me," Gabriel mumbled.

"We'll get you the best lawyer," Angel promised. "And I want the details for Peter's daughter. We'll make sure she gets all the medical help she needs. That fool! Why didn't he just ask me!"

"I can't believe you really thought Cheep was a killer, sis," Cassidy smirked.

"He has that tear drop tattoo!" Billie exclaimed.

Cheep bit his lip. "I actually biro that on each day. And the others. I'm scared of needles."

15

After Wiggles escorted Gabriel to jail, where he assured me he had the nicest en suite room available, Gilbert and I said our goodbyes to Angel and her family.

Gilbert's goodbyes were reluctant and drawn out, and in the end he only left because I reminded him that the Claus family had been managing on their own for some time.

It was as if a spell was broken as he realised that he had not been present for at least one meal and several rounds of hot chocolate.

With that idea firmly in mind, we headed back to Claus Cottage.

The snow was falling in heavy drops and it was hard going stomping a path through the streets.

"Oh Santa help me!" Gilbert exclaimed.

"What is it?"

"I left my measuring cups!"

I frowned at him. "You took our measuring cups with you?"

"I carry them with me always. What would I do if I was

out and about and had to make a hot chocolate for someone?"

"Use a spoon?"

He gasped as if I had suggest he simply buy one.

"I'll have to go back," he said.

"Now?" I asked. "Come on, let's get home and then you can take one of the sleighs."

He shook his head. "I'll be fine. You go home and tell everyone not to fear, Gilbert will be home soon!"

I shrugged. I didn't want to leave him to go off on his own, but the cold was already penetrating through my coat. I wanted to get indoors and warm.

We said our goodbyes and I made the rest of the walk to Claus Cottage as quick as I could.

Father Christmas opened the front door before I had reached it, and ushered me inside. I was touched by his care, until I realised that there was a sound coming from the den that I didn't like at all.

"What's wrong?" I asked, as I climbed out of my winter boots and ran into the den.

My instincts had been correct. The noise was one I hadn't heard in some time, but would never forget.

My sister was crying.

"August?" I cried, and I ran to her and knelt in front of her lap. "What is it? Is Jeb okay?"

"Jeb's fine, dear," Mrs Claus' voice came from behind me. I turned and saw that she was cradling my baby nephew in her arms. He was fast asleep.

"What's happened?" I asked.

"Sit down, dear," Mrs Claus said, and I realised that her own voice was shaky with tears.

Father Christmas appeared in the doorway, dressed for

the outdoors, and with a look of grim determination on his face.

"You all stay here. Understand?" He asked. His booming voice demanded attention and I found myself nod my agreement, even as I didn't know what I was agreeing to.

He gave me a gruff nod and left the room, and then the front door slammed behind him.

"I don't understand," I said.

Mrs Claus took a deep breath. "Holly, we've just had the most awful call. It's Gilbert."

"He's hurt?" I asked. I knew I shouldn't have let him return to Holiday Haven without me!

Mrs Claus shook her head. August's sobs grew louder.

"He's been kidnapped."

THE END

Pre-order your copy of YULE BE SORRY, the next book in the Christmas Mysteries series, now!

CHRISTMAS MYSTERY BONUSES

Help yourself to a festive fun pack, available exclusively at:

https://dl.bookfunnel.com/9ckxf7kcfh

Ho-ho-hope you enjoy it!

Mona x

ABOUT THE AUTHOR

Mona Marple is a lover of all things book-related. When she isn't working on her next release, she's probably curled up somewhere warm reading a good story.

Mona is a fan of all things festive and is looking forward to adding to the Christmas Cozy Mystery series over the years. Her other cozy mysteries include the Waterfell Tweed series, the Mystic Springs paranormal series, the co-written A Witch In Time paranormal series, and the Mexican Mysteries series.

Mona lives in Nottinghamshire, England with her bread baking husband, her always-singing daughter, and their pampered Labradoodle, Coco. In fact, Mona's online reader group were a big part of persuading Mona's husband to welcome Coco into their home!